By DAVID C. DAWSON

For the Love of Luke
Love Wins

Published by DSP Publications:
THE DELINGPOLE MYSTERIES
The Necessary Deaths
The Deadly Lies

Published by DREAMSPINNER PRESS
www.dreamspinnerpress.com

FOR THE LOVE OF LUKE

DAVID C. DAWSON

DREAMSPINNER
PRESS

Published by

DREAMSPINNER PRESS

5032 Capital Circle SW, Suite 2, PMB# 279, Tallahassee, FL 32305-7886 USA
www.dreamspinnerpress.com

Trade Paperback ISBN: 978-1-64080-781-5
Digital ISBN: 978-1-64080-780-8
Library of Congress Control Number: 2018936990
Trade Paperback published October 2018
v. 1.0

Printed in the United States of America

This paper meets the requirements of
ANSI/NISO Z39.48-1992 (Permanence of Paper).

This book is dedicated to Tinyue Liu,
a wonderful man who gave me an enormous amount of guidance
on a particular subject core to the plot of this book.

CHAPTER 1

RUPERT PENDLEY-EVANS had not expected to find the body of a naked man lying on a bathroom floor that evening. But for Rupert Pendley-Evans, life had a habit of taking odd turns.

HE GUIDED his 1200cc motorbike through the gap between the lines of London's Sunday evening traffic and stopped at the junction. The journey back from his parents' estate in rural Buckinghamshire was taking longer than usual. To pass the time, he planned his evening ahead. He would take a shower to wash away the grime of the journey, followed by a glass of chilled pinot grigio.

The lights changed, and the traffic began to move. Rupert's thighs hugged tight to the fuel tank of his BMW. He turned the bike past the two lines of slow-moving cars and took the fork in the road for Vauxhall Bridge. It would lead him across the Thames to the south bank of the river and at long last home. He twitched the throttle, the engine roared, and the bike accelerated up the outside lane, past yet another line of stationary traffic. Rupert glanced to his right as he reached the middle of the bridge. The last rays of July sun silhouetted the upstream London skyline of Battersea and chic Chelsea. It was good to be back in the metropolis after his dutiful two-day visit to the family seat, in the tiny village of Middle Claydon.

He concentrated on the road before him, the final mile of his journey. Ahead, on the south bank of the river, stood the offices of MI6, home to Britain's secret service. It was housed in an imposing piece of postmodern architecture made famous by several appearances in James Bond films. The setting sun glinted orange on the smoked-glass windows, giving the building a warm, rosy glow, belying its true purpose.

As Rupert reached the far end of the bridge, the lights stayed green, and he leaned into the curve of the road. It detoured around Vauxhall bus station and took him past a huddle of modern high-rise apartment blocks funded by Russian investors. He wove the powerful bike in and out of the five lanes of slow-moving traffic and relished the liberty it afforded him. At the third set of lights, he took a left onto Paton Road. The brutal high-rise landscape gave way to a street of elegant Edwardian villas. The rows of shabby front doors and grimy windows were evidence of a former era of long-faded grandeur. Rupert was resigned to the thought one day they too would be swept away by developers in pursuit of tax-free profits.

Rupert slowed the bike to twenty miles an hour. The street became a narrow corridor, and he was hemmed in on both sides by rows of parked cars. Halfway down, he slowed the bike to a crawl and turned sharply onto the forecourt of number 54. He stopped in front of one of the bay windows of the double-fronted Edwardian villa and cut the engine.

He fumbled with the buckle on his chin strap. When he at last removed the crash helmet, the fresh breeze cooled his matted hair, and he breathed a sigh of relief. It had been a long journey. He kicked down the bike's side stand but stayed seated in the saddle. Even though his home was less than half a mile from the bustle of the Vauxhall traffic interchange, it was quiet and peaceful. Rupert listened to the birds singing in the trees on either side of the street. In this tranquil spot, he could fool himself the polluted London air was somehow purer.

The city was in the middle of an English heat wave, and Rupert's leather jeans clung to his thighs with sweat. He looked forward to stripping off and standing under the shower. He stood up, dismounted the bike, and took off his gauntlets. He unzipped his heavy leather jacket, and the evening air cooled his sweat-soaked T-shirt. Rupert unhooked his small overnight bag from its mounting points on the fuel tank and strode to the front door. He punched in the security code and entered the communal hallway of the house.

Number 54 Paton Road was divided into three apartments, each with its own front door. There were two smaller apartments on the ground floor and a third spanning the whole of the upper floor of the house. The apartments all shared the communal entrance hall. A grand, sweeping staircase led to the floor above. Rupert stood outside the front door of number 54a and fumbled in the pocket of his leather jacket for his key.

As soon as he entered the apartment, he sensed something was wrong. There was a strange, musty smell, and he could hear the sound of water running somewhere in the semidarkness beyond. He dropped his overnight bag on the floor, set his crash helmet on the oak hall table, and walked down the corridor leading to the back of the apartment.

The sound of running water grew louder as he approached his open bedroom door. Standing on the threshold, he could see why. The ceiling was bowed, and a steady stream of water poured down onto the polished wooden floorboards below.

Rupert cursed and ran back up the hallway to retrieve a bucket from the hall cupboard. He returned to the bedroom and placed the bucket under the stream of water. He watched it fill with alarmingly rapidity and cursed again.

Rupert had never met the new resident upstairs at number 54c Paton Road. He knew it had changed hands a few months ago, while he was away working for four weeks in the Middle East. He had planned to introduce himself when he returned, but somehow he never found the time. Rupert wished it could have been in better circumstances.

He went out of the apartment to the main staircase and sprinted up the stairs two at a time. The half-glazed door of number 54c was directly in front of him. Rupert rang the bell. After a short pause, he banged hard on the door for good measure. When he still got no response, he tried the doorknob to confirm the door was locked. He pressed his ear to the glass and listened intently. He could hear the sound of running water After banging on the door one last time, he stood back and breathed heavily. Perhaps the tenant had fallen asleep in the bath. Perhaps he had drowned.

Rupert raised his hand and felt the solid wood frame of the door. It would take a lot to open it His only option was to break the door's beautiful stained glass panel. He looked around. To his left was a jumble of flattened cardboard boxes, some discarded packing materials, and three full refuse sacks piled against the wall. He needed something that would help him break the glass safely. On the right, tucked in the corner, was a black metal fire extinguisher. Perfect. Rupert picked it up and tested its weight in his hands. Holding it horizontally, he rested its base against the panel. It was a shame to destroy the glass, he thought. But it was a choice between that and a collapsed bedroom ceiling.

The glass gave way with a satisfying crack. Rupert set down the fire extinguisher and picked up a piece of the discarded packaging material. He wrapped it around his hand and cleared shards of glass from the gaping hole in the door. He reached in cautiously and felt for the catch. It turned easily, and the door swung open. Rupert stepped over the broken glass into the hallway of number 54c.

A series of white spotlights in the ceiling illuminated the corridor. Their light reflected off the white walls of the hallway. The sound of running water was loud and came from a doorway down the corridor. He strode down the hallway and stood on the threshold of the bathroom at number 54c. That was when he saw the body.

The man was naked, lying prostrate on the floor. Water from the overflowing bath lapped around him. Rupert stepped into the bathroom, turned off the water, and crouched down beside the body. He lifted the man's arm and felt for a pulse. The man was alive but unconscious. Rupert reached into the pocket of his leather jacket for his mobile.

"Hello? Ambulance please." While he waited to be connected, Rupert assessed the situation. The man's head rested at the foot of the washbasin, his feet stretched out toward the doorway. His short, curly black hair was matted with congealed blood. Some of it turned the pool of water in which he lay a sickening red. The man looked to be about thirty years old and well over six feet tall. He had an athletic, muscular build. Rupert leaned forward to take a closer look at the head wound. He noticed the man's well-defined cheekbones and his perfect, kiss-shaped lips. Pretty cute, all in all.

Before he could get too distracted, a voice in his ear announced he was connected to the ambulance service.

"Hello? Yes, my name's Rupert Pendley-Evans. I'm at apartment 54c Paton Road, in Vauxhall. It's the one upstairs to mine. There's a guy here unconscious with a head wound. I think he slipped and fell in the bathroom."

Rupert gave his details and as much information about the unknown man as he could provide. He ended the call, stood up, and took a couple of bath towels from a shelf in the corner. He knelt on the floor and did his best to wrap them around the motionless naked body. The man stirred, sending small ripples of movement across his muscular shoulders. He tried to pull himself up and groaned loudly.

"Hey, fella," said Rupert. He leaned close to the man's well-defined cheekbones. "Don't try to move just yet. Looks like you've had a helluva bang on the head."

The man whispered something, and Rupert leaned closer.

"I can't hear you," said Rupert. "Don't worry, the ambulance is on its way."

"I'm freezing," whispered the kiss-shaped lips. The man's body shook in a spasm of shivering to confirm the statement.

Rupert leaned across and massaged the broad back and shoulders. He hoped it would stimulate the man's circulation. A set of long black eyelashes flickered open and revealed dark brown eyes.

"Who are you?" asked the man.

Rupert paused before he replied; the eyes held him captivated with their intensity.

"Hey, welcome back," said Rupert with a sense of relief. "My name's Rupert. I'm your guardian angel from the apartment downstairs. An apartment that's now flooded with your bathwater. What's your name?"

"Luke," replied the man. He grimaced with pain. "Jeez. My head feels like it's been run over by a steamroller. And this water's freezing my balls off."

"I don't think you should move until the ambulance gets here," replied Rupert. "I'm a journalist, not a medic. So I don't really know what I'm doing. And I don't want to risk doing you damage if I try to get you up."

"Then I'll do it myself," replied Luke somewhat petulantly. He levered himself partway into a sitting position and leaned against the side of the bath. He looked at Rupert, and his eyes twinkled with an air of triumph. They partly closed for a moment, and Luke's head lolled from side to side. Rupert caught him before he fell. With difficulty, Rupert held him upright while he sat alongside him and looped his arm over Luke's shoulder.

"Thank you, guardian angel," said Luke, and he rested his head on Rupert's shoulder. He turned his face, and his intense brown eyes stared at Rupert once more.

"What beautiful blue eyes you have," said Luke. He shook his head and winced with pain. "Oh shit. Inappropriate. The stupid American's opened his mouth. Forget I said it." His eyelids drifted shut, and the deep brown eyes disappeared from view.

"Luke? Luke?" said Rupert. "Oh shit. Stay conscious for me." He gently massaged the American's arm and shoulders. "I need you to stay awake until the ambulance comes."

The long black eyelashes flickered, and Luke reopened his eyes.

"That's better," said Rupert. "Stay with me. You've had a head injury. You've got to keep awake. Talk to me. What's your last name?"

"Diamond. Luke Diamond." The long black eyelashes flickered shut. Rupert massaged Luke's shoulders again.

"Hey, Luke Diamond," said Rupert. "Don't drift off. Have you got any family I can contact? Is there a friend I should call?"

Luke slowly turned his head from side to side. "Don't bother." He leaned his head back against the side of the bath. "You don't need to call anyone. Okay?"

Before Rupert could reply, a door buzzer sounded insistently.

"That'll be the ambulance," said Rupert. "Is your entry phone by the front door?"

Luke said nothing but nodded his head.

"I'm going to lay you back on the floor for a moment," said Rupert. "Don't try to get up again. And don't go to sleep."

He gently lowered Luke onto the tiled floor of the bathroom. He reached up to the rail beside the bath, pulled down another towel, and wrapped it around the American's body. Luke mumbled something indistinct, and Rupert leaned in close to hear.

"What was that?" asked Rupert gently.

"I meant what I said," repeated Luke. "You have beautiful eyes." He stared intently at Rupert and sighed. "But you should keep away, handsome blue-eyed Englishman. I know I'm just trouble." The rosebud lips curved upward into a smile.

"I don't believe that for a second." Rupert stood and looked down at Luke. "Don't go away now," he said and headed out of the bathroom to let in the ambulance crew.

CHAPTER 2

THE DOOR of the boathouse creaked open, and the beam of a flashlight shone around the darkness of the interior. After a few moments, the bluish glow settled on a light switch fixed to the wall on the right of the door. A young man entered and walked across the wooden floor. He flipped the switch, and the fluorescent lights suspended from the roof beams flickered and hummed into life.

He walked back to the door, pulled it shut, and locked it. After removing the key and carefully placing it on the floor to the side of the door, he looked up at the roof beams and used the flashlight to confirm his memory of their layout. Satisfied, he removed the rucksack from his back and set it down on the floor.

The young man wore a smart pair of black trousers and a white shirt, on top of which was a blue sweatshirt. It bore the logo London University in white lettering on its front. He wore a pair of earphones attached to a small electronic device fixed on his belt loop.

He sat down cross-legged on the floor and unbuckled the canvas cover of the rucksack. He reached into the bag and took out a coil of rope, a small, squat candle, and a box of matches. The rope he placed to one side. Then he put the candle on the floor in front of him and used the matches to light it.

The young man closed his eyes, placed the palms of his hands on the floor in front of him, and leaned in toward the flickering candle. He began to chant a series of phrases. Slowly and quietly at first, his mutterings virtually inaudible. The incoherent chant became faster and faster. All the while, the young man rocked on his hands, backward and forward, in front of the candle.

After several minutes of rapid chanting and rocking, he stopped, straightened his back, and clapped his hands three times. He opened his eyes wide, leaned forward, and put the palm of his right hand on top of the candle to extinguish the flame. He looked around the interior of the boathouse for a few moments and rubbed the palms of his hands together.

The young man stood up and walked the length of the boathouse to pick up a stepladder that leaned against the wall at the far end. He walked back to where he had sat and set the stepladder beneath a roof beam. He bent down and gathered up the coil of rope, then set his foot on the first rung of the stepladder with the rope thrown across his shoulder.

The stepladder rocked slightly as he climbed to the upper steps. The young man reached to the beam above his head and threw the coil of rope over it. He pulled down on the free end and took up the slack. Carefully, he stood upright on the stepladder, pulled on the rope until the noose he had created at the other end was against his neck, and adjusted its length.

He let the coiled end of the rope drop to the ground. He made one last adjustment to the height of the noose and climbed back down the stepladder. Once he'd retrieved the coil of rope, he carried it over to an iron ring set into the brick wall of the boathouse. He passed the free end of the rope through the ring, carefully took up the slack on the rope, and tied a double loop to secure it.

For one last time, he walked back to the stepladder, climbed to the top, and assessed the height of the noose. Satisfied, he placed the noose over his head and tightened it around his neck. With his right hand, he made the sign of the cross in front of him.

Then he kicked away the ladder.

THE HEAVYSET man walked briskly along the bank of the River Thames. His thick-soled Army boots crunched on the gravel footpath. It was after ten at night, and there was no one else around.

He approached the side door of the university boathouse and set down the heavy canvas bag he had been carrying. From the pocket of his blue overalls, he pulled out a large metal ring of keys. He flicked them over in his hand, until he found the one he was looking for. The key slipped into the lock and turned easily. The man reached into the canvas bag at his feet and pulled out a pair of blue latex gloves.

He put on the gloves, pushed the door open, and surveyed the scene in front of him. Sighing, he stepped inside and carefully closed and locked the door. He looked to his right, bent down, and retrieved the key the young suicide victim had laid there earlier. Putting the key in his pocket, he stood and strode across the floor of the boathouse to the corpse. He lifted one of the suspended figure's arms and felt its pulse.

After a little over a minute, he dropped the arm, reached into the pocket of his overalls, pulled out a mobile phone, and called a number. While he waited, he walked across to a small black plastic globe mounted on the wall and gently pulled it from its mounting. He walked back to his canvas bag and crouched down on his haunches. A voice spoke in the earpiece of the phone.

"Yes, I'm at Chiswick now," the man responded. "The boy used the boathouse just as we planned. I've retrieved the camera. Did you get everything?"

The man shoved the black plastic globe into his canvas bag.

"Yes, it's complete," said the voice on the other end. "We witnessed the event. It was exactly as scripted. No deviations. Please send my congratulations to the doctors. The procedure is flawless. It's now time to apply it to a larger cast of characters."

The man pressed a button on the monitor in his hand. The screen revealed an image of the interior of the boathouse, showing the moment the young man had entered fifty minutes before.

"Of course," said the man. "That goes without saying. Pass my gratitude and condolences to Mr. and Mrs. Templeton. Their son proved himself a worthy sacrifice to the battle."

He turned and looked back at the boathouse.

"I'll clean house here. Then I'll come back with the video of the event for the doctors to see. They'll be very pleased with their work."

CHAPTER 3

RUPERT FLEXED his aching limbs and yawned. The couch had given him an uncomfortable night's sleep. But with the remains of the bedroom ceiling collapsed on his bed, he had little choice. He looked at his watch. It was 6:00 a.m. Rupert shoved back the covers and sat up. There was little point in lying in discomfort any longer. His neck was stiff, his back was stiff, and there was a bruise on his forehead where he had rolled off the couch onto the coffee table in the night.

All because of that bloody Yank upstairs. All the same, he was worth a second look.

Rupert stretched out his long legs and looked down at the bulge in his boxers. Early-morning wood, he wondered? Or stirrings brought on by memories of last night's encounter? Absently, he scratched himself and planned out his day. He had to be at the editorial meeting at 9:00 a.m. It was in the heart of the BBC's news operation at the top of Regent's Street. Late morning, he would head down to Soho to record a commentary for his next documentary film. He decided he would walk to the sound studio, hang around after, and get a bite to eat in Balans restaurant. In the afternoon, he had a routine briefing at the Metropolitan Police headquarters in New Scotland Yard. It was on the edge of Vauxhall, so he would head straight home after and try to sort out the mess in his bedroom.

He picked up his phone and checked the messages. There was just one, from an unknown number.

Thanks for coming to my rescue. Sorry I fucked up your apartment. I'll pay for the damage. Luke XOXO

Last night, Rupert had written his number on a piece of paper and given it to the paramedics for Luke, as they carried him to the ambulance. At the thought of Luke, his crotch stirred again. He stood up and headed for the bathroom. Time for a shower. A cold one.

"MORNIN', SWEETHEART. You look like shit."

The woman's voice had a strong East End accent. It cut through the early-morning quiet of the newsroom like the voice of a stallholder at Billingsgate fish market. Rupert strolled across the vast open floor of the BBC's news operation toward a diminutive woman. She had long peroxide-blonde hair and held her arms outstretched to him.

"Morning, Sandra darling," said Rupert and embraced her. "Love you too, sweetie."

"Mmm," replied Sandra. "Love the smell of yer leather jacket first fing in the mornin'. Gets me all moist for the day." She reached up and kissed him on both cheeks.

Rupert laughed.

"It's good to be back in reality, after the last two days," he said.

"Oh yeah," said Sandra, "'ow were Lord and Lady Pendley-Evans? You were up at the estate, weren't yer? Your mum still shaggin' that new gardener, is she?"

Rupert set his crash helmet down on the desk next to Sandra's and slipped the rucksack off his back. He raised a finger to his lips.

"Shh, darling," he said. "That's a malicious, unfounded piece of gossip. Don't go spreading it around in a newsroom."

He winked at Sandra.

"Anyway," he continued. "The jury's out on Juan's sexuality."

"Oh yeah?" said Sandra. She sat down at her desk and turned to her laptop. "Gonna 'ave a pop at 'im yerself are yer? You didn't tell me he was Spanish. Fancy a bit of chorizo meself."

"He's Argentinian." Rupert unzipped his leather jacket, slipped it off his shoulders, and hung it on the back of his chair. "I'll let you know if he swings your way rather than mine."

He sat on the BBC standard-issue swivel chair at his desk and groaned as he rubbed the back of his neck and twisted in the chair to try to get comfortable.

Sandra turned to look at him.

"What's wrong wiv you? Been shaggin' all night again, 'ave yer?"

"I wish," replied Rupert. He told her about his encounter with Luke and the events of the night before.

"An' you didn't get to shag 'im? Is that why you're so fuckin' miserable?"

Rupert sighed and switched on his computer. "It's not always about sex, Sandra." He turned and raised an eyebrow at her.

"Rupert Pendley-Evans, you're so full of shit this mornin'," she said. "We've been workin' together 'ow long? Two years? Every other mornin', all I ever 'ear about is your latest conquest. You've had more men than I've even dated."

Sandra cupped her hands under her chin and rested her elbows on the desk. She tilted her head and fluttered her eyelashes.

"But of course, and I quote the *Daily Mail* here," Sandra continued, "the BBC's latest onscreen reporter, The Hon. Rupert Pendley-Evans, is handsome in that quintessentially English aristocratic way. His tall, athletic build gives him a dominant presence. His wavy brown hair frames a strong, angular face. His piercing blue eyes—"

She ducked as Rupert threw one of his leather motorbike gloves at her. She caught it and clutched it to her chest.

"Oh, Rupert," she teased. "A piece of your clothin'. If only it had been a pair of your boxers. I'd get a bleedin' fortune for 'em on eBay."

"Enough," said Rupert. "I can't help it if the tabloids won't take me seriously."

Sandra threw the glove back at him, and he stuffed it inside his crash helmet.

"Are you comin' to the briefin' in ten minutes?" asked Sandra. She turned back to her laptop. "I reckon Eileen's got 'er iron knickers on again today. She 'ad a real go at me when she came in this mornin'. Reckoned my edit of the refugee story was too rushed. She must be hormonal again."

Eileen Jones was the editor in chief of BBC News and Current Affairs, a formidable woman with a razor-sharp mind and a fiery Welsh tongue.

The screen on Rupert's computer flashed into life, and he typed in his name and password.

"Perhaps she's just worried about the Parliamentary Select Committee she's got to address this afternoon," he said.

Sandra stopped typing and swiveled her chair back to Rupert.

"You stickin' up for 'er now?" she asked. "After iron-knickers Eileen ripped your bollocks off in front of everyone last month over your Royal abdication cock-up?"

Rupert shivered as he remembered the verbal dressing down Eileen Jones had meted out. In his documentary on the future of the Royal Family, he'd speculated on the threat to the House of Windsor from the present government. He suggested a president might take the place of the monarch, if the Palace did nothing and remained complacent.

"I'll be there," he answered. "I just hope she's forgiven me by now. I need to get back onto current affairs again. I'm getting bored on the news desk."

THE SMALL windowless conference room was packed with nearly thirty journalists, producers, and picture editors. At 9:00 a.m. sharp, Eileen Jones strode into the room.

"Right," she said and dropped her laptop on the table. "I've got to warn you, I'm not in the best of moods this morning. I've got Herbert bloody Humble cross-questioning me on the Parliamentary Select Committee this afternoon."

Rupert looked across the table at Sandra and raised an eyebrow. She responded by crossing her eyes.

"We'll go through the news agenda in a minute," continued Eileen. She put on a pair of reading glasses and looked down at her laptop. "But before we do, I've got a couple of staffing arrangements I want to announce."

The atmosphere in the room chilled immediately. Ever since the recent change of minister at the Department for Culture, talk about cuts to the BBC's guaranteed, state-backed funding had been flying around in the press. Eileen Jones looked up and peered over her reading glasses at the pairs of anxious eyes staring at her.

"That got your attention," she said with a smile. "Don't panic, ladies and gentlemen. You've still got jobs." She looked around at the sea of faces. "For the moment," she added and looked across at Rupert. "Mr. Pendley-Evans."

Twenty-nine pairs of eyes turned to stare at Rupert.

"Despite last month's fiasco, and the chairman having to grovel to the Palace, I want to put you back on current affairs."

Rupert clenched his fist under the conference room table in a small personal victory celebration.

"Thank you, Eileen," said Rupert. "Do you want me to carry on with the refugee story?"

Eileen Jones shook her head. "No, I'll leave Bob and Gemma on that." She looked across at Sandra. "And try to do a better cut on the pictures next time, Sandra. It's not a bloody wedding video you're editing."

Eileen turned to Rupert again. Sandra pulled a face at the news editor and slumped back in her seat.

"Rupert, I want you to work up a piece on these suicide statistics." She held up a large spiral-bound document. "There's a new report out from the charity Manwatch," she continued. "It's called 'Desperate Britain.' Seems like the suicide rate, particularly among young men, has risen steeply in the last four years."

Eileen Jones looked over her glasses at Rupert. "I think it could be right up your street."

Rupert wrinkled his nose as if someone had just farted. "What the hell's Manwatch?" he asked. "It sounds a bit daytime to me. Can't you give it to the kids on *Hello Britain!*?"

Eileen took off her reading glasses and stared hard at him. "In my opinion," she said coldly, "there's a potentially very good political piece in this. Don't forget. It's four years since this heartless government came to power. The rise in suicides, and the government's appalling record on social care, will not be unconnected."

She put her glasses back on and looked down at her laptop. "Mr. Pendley-Evans. You might be 'the BBC's roguish reporter' in the eyes of the *Daily Mail*. But another cock-up like last month, and I'll have you writing obituaries in the corner of the stationery cupboard."

Rupert looked across at Sandra, who crossed her eyes at him again.

"Of course, Eileen," he said. "When do you want it?"

"When you've got a decent story, Mr. Pendley-Evans," replied the news editor. "So don't go shooting your bolt prematurely."

She looked up and surveyed the other faces around the table.

"Now," she continued, "the other staffing changes."

"GOING TO join me in a celebratory coffee?" asked Rupert as Sandra emerged from the airless conference room an hour later.

"You're a jammy bugger," replied Sandra. They walked down the corridor together to the on-site coffee shop. "No one else could use their get-out-of-jail card that quick. Just because you're well connected with royalty. Old iron knickers reckons she's got to keep you sweet, otherwise you'll be off to Sky Television."

"Fuck off, Sandra," replied Rupert. "If you overlook last month's little hiccup—"

"Little?" squealed Sandra. "When the chairman has to go rimming the Royal household? It's hardly little."

"If you overlook last month," continued Rupert, ignoring her interruption. "I've had two major news stories this year that led to Parliamentary reviews. Then, of course, there's my Royal Television Society award last year—"

He stopped as his phone vibrated in his pocket. He pulled out the mobile and answered the call.

"Hello? Yes, it is. Thank you." He turned to Sandra and motioned her to move away. She leaned against the corridor wall and grinned broadly.

"Sandra," said Rupert with exasperation. "Will you go away? It's—hello?" He turned as a voice sounded in the receiver.

"Hi, Luke," Rupert continued. "How are you doing?"

Sandra threw back her head and laughed.

"Maybe you can make your lovely Yank more than a one-night stand, darlin'," she whispered loudly. "Unlike all the others."

Rupert turned and glowered at her. Sandra responded by folding her arms and shaking her head. Rupert turned away and cupped his hand around the phone to speak quietly.

"Sure I can," he said. "Did they say you can leave now? If you like, I can get a taxi for you." He furrowed his brow as he listened for a few moments before speaking again. "Well, if you're sure. I'll drop in when I get home later. See if you need anything."

"I'd get some condoms if I was you" came Sandra's voice from behind him. Rupert spun around and glowered at her. He raised a finger to his lips.

"I meant, like food or something," he continued into the phone. "A curry, or a Chinese. Or I can cook something if you want. I make a mean chili."

Sandra started making kissing noises. She hugged her arms around her waist and twisted her hips from side to side.

"No, don't worry about that," said Rupert, turning away from his tormentor. "I just need to get the decorators in to sort it out."

He listened for a few moments.

"No, honestly. It'll just go through on insurance. Don't worry. It'll be fine. Okay. See you later. Cheers."

He ended the call, shoved the phone in the pocket of his jeans, and stood facing Sandra with his arms folded.

"You little shit, Sandra Giles."

"Oh come off it, Rupert Pendley-Evans. You can't wait to get 'is pants off. Mind you," she continued, "it's not goin' to be a bundle of laughs when you've 'alf yer bleedin' ceiling on the bed wiv yer."

Sandra cocked her head. "Not unless that's your particular kink."

Rupert sighed. "I rang the cleaners first thing this morning. They can't come round until Thursday. I'm going to have to shift the worst of it myself. Unless—" He took a step forward and placed his hands on Sandra's shoulders. "Would you by any chance...?"

Sandra shook her head.

"You must be bleedin' jokin', Rupert Pendley-Evans. What do you take me for? Some kinda skivvy?"

"Oh come on, Sandra. I'll cook you a meal."

Sandra laughed. "You're already doin' that for sex on a stick. 'A mean chili' is what I 'eard you offer 'im. You don't want me there as well. I certainly don't wanna be the fuckin' gooseberry."

"Well, maybe not tonight," agreed Rupert. "But tell you what. I know you've been angling to go to Blitz Club 2 for ages. If you help me out tonight, I'll take us there on Friday."

"Bloody 'ell, Pendley-Evans, you're pretty fuckin' desperate, aren't yer?" She raised a recently plucked eyebrow and looked at him quizzically. "You can't seriously get us into Blitz Club 2, can yer?"

Rupert held his hands palm up in front of him, like a magician who had pulled a rabbit from a hat. "Oh sure. I'm on the guest list anytime I want. Being a *Daily Mail* pinup offers certain advantages. Is it a deal?"

Sandra shrugged. "Fuckin' journalists. I can see 'ow you worm your way into places. Okay. As long as I get to meet the hunky Yank, and you don't introduce me as yer bleedin' cleanin' lady, I'll do it."

It was a constant source of amusement to Rupert how Sandra was desperate to get into any and all of the fashionable clubs in London. He never understood their attraction.

"Anyway," continued Sandra. "I've always thought your place needed a woman's touch. I'll be at yours for six thirty tonight. And you better 'ave some rubber gloves ready for me. These nails cost a bleedin' fortune."

CHAPTER 4

"FUCK ME, Rupert, you can't sleep 'ere. Or do anything else 'ere for that matter."

Sandra looked around the devastation of Rupert's flood-damaged bedroom. Most of the ceiling had collapsed, exposing wooden rafters and dangling electrical cables. The bed was covered with broken sections of plasterboard and puddles of dirty water. Jagged brown circles stained two elegant Chinese rugs on either side of the bed. A large chrome-framed mirror had fallen from the wall and smashed across the brass bedhead.

Rupert leaned against the bedroom doorway, his hands shoved deep into the pockets of his leather biker's jacket. The devastation was even worse than he remembered it from that morning. It looked like he was going to have another fitful night's sleep.

"So I'm sleeping on the couch again tonight." He sighed. "The mattress and bedding must be soaked. I'm going to have to replace everything. And it stinks of damp."

He wrinkled his nose and turned to Sandra, who stood beside him.

"I don't think you need to put on the rubber gloves, sweetheart," Rupert continued. "Do you fancy a drink or three, now you're here?"

Sandra slipped her arm through his and squeezed tight.

"You're supposed to be cooking for a special someone, remember? You can't get too smashed if you're seein' yer dishy fella."

"Er, hi?"

The voice came from above their heads. Rupert and Sandra looked up to see a man's face peering down through a gaping hole in the ceiling.

"Blimey, Rupert," whispered Sandra. "'E's fuckin' gorgeous! An' that bandage on 'is 'ead makes 'im look so vulnerable. I could—"

"Hi, Luke!" called out Rupert to interrupt her before she said any more. "How's your head? You'd better watch your step up there. I don't want to play the hero two days in a row."

A broad grin lit up Luke's face.

"Don't worry. I'm holding on real tight up here!" he replied. "Can I come down to see the mess I've made?"

Before Rupert could reply, Sandra opened her mouth to speak. "'Course you can, love! We're about to crack open a bottle of somethin'. Come and take the weight off yer plates."

"Plates?" asked Luke. He looked puzzled.

"Plates of meat—feet," replied Rupert. "It's Cockney rhyming slang. Sandra claims to be a Cockney, even though she comes from Chigwell, which makes her nothing more than an Essex girl."

Sandra gave him a sharp jab in his ribs. Rupert turned to wrestle her into a headlock.

"Ow, Rupert! You fucker!" Sandra's voice came from somewhere below his waist.

"This is Sandra Giles," announced Rupert to Luke. "Picture editor extraordinaire from BBC Special Reports." Rupert continued to resist Sandra's struggles. "She spends all day in a darkened room watching dodgy TV. Which is why she's got a filthy mouth on her when they finally release her into the daylight."

He let Sandra go from the headlock. She turned to kick him in the shin and then looked up to the ceiling. Luke was still peering down at them with a bemused expression on his face.

"And you've already met The Hon. Rupert Pendley-Evans. Second son of Lord and Lady Pendley-Evans," said Sandra. "Though fuck knows why they call 'im 'on'rable when he treats 'is friends like this."

Luke laughed. "He sure was honorable toward me last night. I'll come down and say hi properly."

He disappeared from view.

Sandra turned and looked up at Rupert. Her face was thunderous with fury.

"What the 'ell did you have to do that for?" she said. "You made me look like a right plonker."

"Well, you punched me in the kidney," replied Rupert.

"That's the 'ighest I can reach on you, Rupert Pendley-Evans. You should be grateful it wasn't your manhood I went for. Otherwise you'd be no fuckin' use to lover-boy Luke." She ran her fingers through the strands of her long blonde hair. "And if it turns out he doesn't 'ook up to your particular train, you can always point 'im in my direction. I'd be more than 'appy to attach his couplin' to mine—"

"Hello again," Luke's voice called from down the hallway. "You left your front door open, so I came straight in."

"Sandra!" said Rupert. He looked at her accusingly.

Sandra turned to admire Luke as he approached them down the corridor. "Fuck me," she said. "You're even more gorgeous in the flesh. Oh my God!" She looked at Rupert and winked. "Did I just say that out loud?"

Rupert eased Sandra aside, stepped forward as Luke reached the entrance to the bedroom, and held out his hand in greeting. Luke clasped it, and they shook hands formally.

"Bloody 'ell, you two," said Sandra. She looked first at Rupert and then longingly at Luke. "Are you seriously just going to shake hands? I 'eard that last night—"

"Sandra," said Rupert. "Shut your mouth, will you? It's making a howling gale in here."

"Gee, it's a helluva mess," said Luke. He looked over Rupert's shoulder. "I'm real sorry for causing you so much trouble. Have you got another room to sleep in? For sure this one's out of action."

Rupert shook his head. "Mine's the smallest apartment in the building. It's just the one bedroom. I'm afraid I'm on the couch until the decorators come to fix it up."

"No you're not," replied Luke. "I've got a spare room. You can come sleep in mine. It's the least I can do."

"Oh, but you don't need to—"

"What Rupert's tryin' to say," interrupted Sandra, "is that 'e's very 'appy to take you up on your offer. He'll pack 'is things now and be upstairs in a jiffy."

Luke looked down at Sandra and laughed. "The lady's right, Rupert. You can't sleep here. And if your couch is anything like mine, you'll have a backache for months. My spare room's got a queen-size bed—"

"Ooh, how appropriate," said Sandra. She turned to Rupert. "You'll feel right at home in that."

"All right, all right," said Rupert. He threw his hands in the air in mock surrender. "If I'm honest, I really can't face another night on the couch. I'll happily sleep in your spare room for the next few days. But in return I'm going to cook dinner for you tonight."

"It's a deal," said Luke, and he held out his hand to Rupert.

Sandra shook her head in disbelief. She grabbed Rupert around the waist and shoved him unceremoniously toward Luke.

"For God's sake, Rupert. Give the man a hug at least!" she said.

Rupert put his arms around Luke's shoulders, in part to steady himself, in part because it felt good. He was within kissing distance of the American's lips when Luke's body tensed. He looked into his eyes and could see Luke was uncomfortable with the enforced embrace. Rupert dropped his arms hurriedly and took a step away. To cover the awkwardness of the moment, he took Luke's right hand in his and shook it vigorously.

"Sure, it's a deal," said Rupert. "I'm starving anyway. Sandra and I will get the chili started, so why don't you come back and join us in about an hour—"

"Oh no," said Sandra. She started to walk away from them down the corridor. "I've got me roots to do tonight. I'm not 'angin' round 'ere playin' bleedin' gooseberry."

She opened the front door, turned to look at Rupert and Luke, and wagged her finger at them.

"You two sort yerselves out. 'Ave a nice evenin', boys."

The door slammed behind her, and its sound echoed down the corridor. Rupert slumped against the wall and sighed.

"I'm so sorry about Sandra," he began. "She has a habit of speaking her mind. Even if—"

"Hey, don't say sorry," interrupted Luke. "I think she's great. If anyone should say sorry, it's me."

He took a step toward Rupert and laid a hand tentatively on his shoulder. Rupert was unsure how to respond after the mixed message he had received from the fumbled embrace. He knew what he wanted to do. The gathering grasp of Luke's hand on his shoulder, and the warm rush of Luke's breath against his cheek, sent his memory flicking back to the night before. He recalled the exquisite beauty of Luke's naked form, lying vulnerable on the bathroom floor. The taut, ebony shine of the American's skin, and the seductive sculpture of his motionless torso. Rupert slowly extended an arm, rested his hand on Luke's waist, and waited.

Luke's eyes scanned Rupert's face for a few moments. He sighed, and the intoxicating rush of the American's breath brushed against Rupert's face once more.

"I don't remember too much about last night," Luke began. "But I do remember saying something embarrassing about those beautiful blue eyes of yours. And as I look at them now, I have to say, they're more beautiful than ever."

He slowly pulled Rupert toward him and kissed him gently on the cheek. He rested his forehead against Rupert's and whispered, "Beware, beautiful Englishman. I'm complicated."

RUPERT TURNED down the gas under the pan as the smell of frying onions flooded the narrow galley kitchen of Luke's apartment. He opened the deep drawer below the stove top and searched for a large pan to boil water for the rice.

Luke had persuaded him to transfer the evening's cooking operations to his upstairs apartment. That way they could talk while Luke cleared the clutter from his spare room. Rupert found the unfamiliar kitchen easy to navigate. Cooking pots and utensils were in the place he expected to find them. The cupboards turned up a good supply of quality spices and herbs. It was gratifying to find the American took his food as seriously as Rupert.

Luke appeared at the kitchen doorway, a CD case in either hand.

"Two questions for you. Adele or George Michael? And red or white?"

Rupert straightened up from the drawer. He held a large saucepan in his hand.

"Definitely Adele," he said. "And why don't you open a bottle of red? Then I can use some of it in the chili. We can drink the rest."

"Good plan," replied Luke, and he disappeared from the doorway. A few moments later, the sound of "Home Town," sung by the north London singing legend, drifted through from the living room. Luke reappeared at the kitchen doorway. He held two large glasses of red wine in one hand and an opened bottle in the other.

"Here," he said and handed the bottle to Rupert. "This will liven up the chili tonight. It's an exceptionally fine Syrah I brought back from France last month."

Rupert took the bottle and set it on the counter beside the stove. He retrieved a glass of red wine from Luke and inhaled the bouquet.

"That's very fine indeed," he commented. He took a sip and held the liquid in his mouth for several seconds before he swallowed it. "I'm not sure we should be cooking with it. Where did you say you got it?"

"Oh, sure. Put it in the chili. I've got plenty more. I was staying in Collioure, down in the South West of France. Do you know it?"

"Oh yes, a wonderful place," said Rupert. "I went there when I was a student."

"It is," continued Luke. "I went over the border into Spain for a few days. I wanted to see the coastline on that side of Spain and visit Figueres. You know the place? The Dali museum?"

"Oh yes. Lots of painters have spent time in that region over the years."

"It's a stunning part of the world," said Luke. "The light is somehow different to any I've experienced before. Matisse lived in Collioure. And of course Picasso. It was real inspirational. I'd say almost spiritual."

Rupert held out his glass to Luke.

"Well, you made an excellent choice with the wine. Cheers."

They clinked their glasses together and sipped the ruby-red liquid. Rupert watched Luke close his eyes and roll the wine around in his mouth. His Adam's apple bobbed as he swallowed. A look of what Rupert could only describe as serenity engulfed the American's face. Luke reopened his eyes.

"It's like nectar, isn't it?" The air of serenity remained in Luke's expression as he spoke. "You can taste the sunshine, the clear air, the intensity of the light. That part of Europe is an artist's paradise."

Rupert could see two artworks hanging on the wall of the hallway outside the kitchen. Both canvases were about three foot square and appeared to be part of a larger work. They were dark, brooding pieces; the brushstrokes seemed rapid and angry. Rupert could see no sign of the azure blue Mediterranean light he recalled from the times he had spent in and around the coastal border area of southwest France and Spain.

"I see you brought back some souvenirs with you," he said. "Are they from Spain or France?"

"Neither," replied Luke with a grin. "They're from Vauxhall. Those are my own attempts at art."

"Really?" said Rupert in surprise. He carried his glass out into the hallway, took another sip of wine, and examined the canvases. In the confined corridor, it was difficult to get far enough away to take in the combined composition of the two pieces. Standing close to them, he could sense the furious energy the artist had thrown into their creation.

"They're impressive," said Rupert. "Forbidding, but impressive."

Luke sighed and turned to go back into the living room. "I knew you wouldn't like them."

"I didn't say that," protested Rupert and followed him. "I really find them—" He searched for the right word. "—interesting. They just weren't quite...."

Luke turned to face Rupert at the door to the living room. "But you don't like them, do you? That's a real pity." He raised his hands and gestured to the ceiling. "After we'd eaten, I was going to take you upstairs and show you more. Maybe it's not such a good idea—"

"You have an upstairs?" asked Rupert.

"Sure," replied Luke. "It's my studio. In the converted roof space. There's only a ladder to get up to it. It's a bit rough and ready. But there's lots of light." He grinned at Rupert. "My humble artist's garret. Here's the deal. You cook us a meal, and I'll take you upstairs later."

"Now there's an invitation," said Rupert. He raised his glass to Luke. "Here's to you, the complicated American, with his overflowing bathwater and his paintings in the attic."

CHAPTER 5

THE FLAMES on the five tall candles set in the glass candelabra sputtered and swayed. Rupert carried a heavy iron pot of chili from the kitchen and placed it on the table in front of Luke. The last rays of evening sun had long gone, but a glow of twilight filtered through the large Edwardian window and illuminated the small, square dining room in Luke's apartment. As with all the windows on that balmy evening, Luke had opened them wide to invite in any whisper of a cooling breeze to displace the suffocating heat in the upper part of the house.

"Voilà!" said Rupert. He removed the pot lid and stood back to let Luke admire its contents.

"It smells great!" said Luke. He leaned over the chili and inhaled its aroma. "Your own recipe?"

Rupert put the lid down on a glass mat that protected the polished oak surface of the dining table. He sat opposite Luke, picked up a large serving spoon, and handed it across the table.

"Here, help yourself to some rice," he said. "Yes, sort of. I only learned to cook about ten years ago. When I ran away from home to live with a chef. I survived on vile school dinners and takeouts before that."

"A chef, eh? Your first lover?" asked Luke. He spooned a generous portion of rice onto his plate and handed the spoon to Rupert, who dug deep into the bowl of rice.

"In fact," Rupert continued, "he was the executive chef at the Savoy Hotel in London. A tall German guy with an amazing body and a very fast BMW motorbike. At least, it was fast when he rode it. The first time I watched him cook, I decided I had to learn. He taught me how to improvise recipes and cook with what you've got."

"You ran away from home?" asked Luke.

Rupert sat down and arranged a well-laundered damask napkin on his lap.

"I was eighteen, and I'd recently come out to my parents." He handed his plate to Luke. "It didn't go well."

"What happened?" asked Luke. He piled a generous portion of chili onto Rupert's plate.

"Hey, that's enough for me," said Rupert. He held up his hand before Luke could offload another spoonful. Rupert took the plate back and set it down in front of him.

"Father told me to grow up, and Mother suggested I join the Army. My parents are rather old-fashioned in their outlook on life. They might be Lord and Lady Pendley-Evans, but basically Father's a farmer in deepest Buckinghamshire, and Mother's a farmer's wife. I think I'm the first gay man they've ever met. I expect they'd rather not believe I'm gay."

Luke served himself a portion of chili, placed the serving spoon on a porcelain spoon rest, and replaced the lid of the iron pot. He picked up his fork and tasted the chili.

"Wow, that's a hell-raiser."

Rupert took a bowl of grated cheese and handed it to Luke. "Here. Have some of this."

He looked at the dishes on the table. "Damn," he said. "I forgot the sour cream. Hang on a minute."

Rupert stood up and headed out of the dining room. As he entered the kitchen, a mobile phone on the countertop began to ring. Rupert noticed it was not a modern smartphone, but more like one he had owned more than five years ago.

"Luke," he called. "Your phone's ringing. Do you want me to bring it in?"

Luke appeared at the kitchen door. He walked over to the counter and turned off the phone.

"I'm not in tonight." Luke tossed the phone into a fruit basket at the far end of the kitchen.

"If you don't mind me saying," said Rupert, "that's a really old phone." He picked up a small white porcelain bowl from the countertop and handed it to Luke. "Here's the sour cream."

Luke took the bowl and headed back to the dining room. Rupert followed.

"I'm not big on technology," said Luke. He sat down at the table and served himself a generous helping of cream. "I need a phone to make phone calls, not play dumb games." Rupert felt admonished for owning a smartphone but said nothing as he took the bowl of sour cream from Luke.

"Tell me about the executive chef of the Savoy," continued Luke. "How did you meet him when you were only eighteen?"

"I went to a ghastly public school in London," said Rupert. "I spent my life trying to escape. By the way, a public school actually means a private school when you translate it into American." He looked up at Luke. "As the wonderful Oscar Wilde once put it, we have everything in common with America except our language."

Luke laughed and picked up his glass of wine. "To the chef of the evening. An Englishman who cooks a mean chili. I'm going to be breathing fire tonight at this rate." He took a sip from his glass and placed it back on the table.

"Why do you call them public schools when they're private, anyway?" asked Luke.

"Oh, that's easy," replied Rupert. He tucked into his chili. "Long before there was state funding for schools in England, it was really only the church that set up schools. Rich people set up public schools for those who didn't want to have to belong to any particular religion so their children could be educated. In other words, they were open to the public. The paying public of course," he added.

"History lesson gratefully received." Luke placed his palms together in front of him in mock servitude. "But why was your school so terrible?"

"Partly because I was a boarder," replied Rupert. "I was a long way from home. Or at least it felt that way. And also because I was bullied. Even worse, my parents did nothing about it. My father had gone to the same school, and he said it made a man of him. So he thought it would do the same for me. You see, in those days I was a delicate child who hated rugger and cricket and all these stupid games you have to play at an English public school—"

"Whereas now you're over six foot tall, broad-shouldered, and gym-honed," said Luke with a smile. "What happened along the way?"

"Why thank you, kind sir," said Rupert and waved his arm before him as though at court. He picked up his glass of wine and drank. "This really is an excellent vintage." He set the glass down on the table. "What happened? Like I said, I met the executive chef of the Savoy, and I fell madly in love with him. He was thirteen years older than me. A beautiful man. Successful. Romantically foreign. He was German. And he'd not only succeeded in a foreign country, but he'd also succeeded in a cutthroat profession dominated by the French. Even better, he rode a motorbike and swaggered around in leathers. I was besotted."

Rupert scooped up a forkful of chili and rice and shoved it in his mouth. He looked across at Luke, who gazed at him with a frown on his face.

"Are you still in love with him?" asked Luke.

Rupert swallowed and shook his head.

"He's long gone from my life. We only lived together for a year. But he opened my eyes to everything that I'd been missing—"

"You mean sex?" asked Luke.

Rupert shook his head. "I was already getting that. That's one thing I did learn at public school." He sighed as he thought back to his teenage years at the Henry Royal School in Westminster.

"So it wasn't all bad at school, then?" asked Luke.

A vision of his former teenage self flashed into Rupert's mind. "I'm afraid most of the time it was. You see, although I say it myself, I was a very pretty boy. In those days, my hair was in long blond ringlets, and my skin was smooth and fair. I spent a lot of my time hiding from the older boys who were after me."

"Weren't you flattered?"

"I was terrified. I didn't want to be gay. I wanted to be a man. I wanted my father to be proud of me."

"But weren't you attracted to the other boys?"

"Some of them. But as I say, I was terrified. They'd make a joke about it. And I was the joke. It wasn't funny. They'd say they wanted to screw the batty boy." Rupert set down his fork and sat back in his chair. "I'm sorry. I didn't mean to harp on about this nonsense. It's long gone and there are much nicer things to talk about."

"No, no," said Luke. "Please go on. I'm real interested. How did you survive? Didn't the school do anything?"

"Ha!" said Rupert. He shook his head dismissively. "They knew damn well it was going on. I know that because I told them. But they took the side of the bullies. When I reported it to my housemaster, he just said it was my fault."

Rupert sat forward. He picked up his fork and pointed it at Luke as he imitated his housemaster. "Pendley-Evans. Stop being a sissy and start being a man. If you insist on looking like a girl, with your long blond hair and your girly body, what do you expect? I've seen you hiding in the library when you should be out on the rugger field or going on a cross-country run. You need to man up and show us you're worthy of our school motto: *scientia ac labore.*"

"Which means?"

"Knowledge through hard work," replied Rupert with a snort. "Which was complete rubbish. After all, it wasn't the most academic of schools. Most of the boys were pretty thick. They certainly didn't work hard. But they were rich. A lot of them went on to be bankers, who are the bullies of the City. The rest simply returned home to manage daddy's estate in the country."

"Which I guess is what your father wanted you to do. How did you end up a journalist?" asked Luke.

"It was Christoph. The executive chef of the Savoy. He showed me how I could be anything I wanted to be. That I didn't have to simply do everything Father demanded."

A sudden gust of cold air blew in from the window and extinguished two of the candles in the candelabra. Luke stood up and crossed the dining room to a small oak writing desk. He opened one of the drawers and retrieved a box of matches.

"He sounds like the perfect man," said Luke. He returned to the table and lit the candles again. "How did you meet him? Surely you were locked up in your British boarding school day after day?"

"Once we were sixteen, we got special privileges," explained Rupert. "At weekends we were allowed out without having to wear school uniform, provided we were back by eight in the evening. That's when I discovered the Coleherne. It was a gay pub in Earl's Court. It's long gone now. Renamed the Pembroke. I was sixteen and a half when I first went there. I was completely illegal of course."

"How did you manage to get in on your own?"

"I didn't," replied Rupert. "Not everyone stayed inside the Coleherne. A large crowd hung around outside. It was very popular with men in leather. Freddie Mercury had been a regular in the eighties. It was very famous. I'll never forget the first time I went. It was a hot Saturday afternoon in May. I got the District Line Tube at Westminster to Earl's Court. The pub was just down the road from the Tube station. I was terrified. I walked past it on the opposite side of the street to start with. Then I crossed the road and walked past again. There were all these men standing around outside, drinking and laughing. I'd got so scared that I'd decided to walk back to the Tube station. Then I heard this voice behind me."

Luke gestured to Rupert's plate. "Don't let your food get cold, Rupert. I've nearly finished mine, and I'm going to have some more. Is that okay?"

"Of course," said Rupert. He stood up, reached across the table, and removed the lid from the pot of chili. "Am I talking too much again?" he asked as he served Luke. "I'm always doing that. Help yourself to rice."

"No, I didn't mean that," said Luke hurriedly. "I love hearing your story. There's so much I want to know about London. So the voice was Christoph's, was it?"

Rupert sat down and picked up his napkin from the floor where it had fallen. "Yes. He was standing there in his bike leathers, a pint of beer in his hand. I couldn't help noticing how tightly his leathers fitted. They were unzipped to his waist. There were little beads of sweat, glistening on his chest. It was a glorious sight. I could feel my cock hardening by the second."

"But I thought you didn't feel anything for the boys at school. How come you were suddenly attracted to this man?"

"No, I didn't say I didn't feel anything for them. I said I didn't want to feel anything." Rupert took a sip from his wine. "But I was certainly attracted to them. I hated being in the communal showers after games. I couldn't look at any of the other boys. I was terrified

I'd get an erection." Rupert put down his wineglass and looked at Luke. "I was ashamed of how I felt. It was miserable. But that day at the Coleherne, in the heat of the afternoon, with all those other men around me, and seeing Christoph standing there—"

He looked across at Luke, who had picked up the bottle of Syrah and refilled Rupert's glass.

"So come on, then," said Rupert. "Now it's your turn. When was the first time you fell in love with a man?"

Luke refilled his own glass and set the bottle back on a silver tablemat. He picked up the glass, took a long drink, and looked across at Rupert.

"I can't remember," he said.

Rupert grinned. "Have there been that many? I'm not surprised."

"No, Rupert," said Luke. "I mean I can't remember. I can't remember anything of my life before I came to London. It's just a blank."

CHAPTER 6

THE MOON hung low in the sky that night. Even with the light pollution in London, it shone brightly—and faintly red. An early harvest moon in July. Rupert stood by the open window and gazed at it, an almost-empty glass of wine in his hand. The wind had dropped, and the atmosphere had become close and stifling once more.

Luke was in the kitchen, clearing up the supper dishes. Pans clanged and crockery rattled as he loaded the dishwasher. Rupert reflected on the one-sidedness of their conversations earlier. When he had enthusiastically talked about his past life and his past encounters, it seemed Luke was genuinely interested and keen to hear more. Rupert was well aware when he became a bore at dinner parties and had long ago learned to ration his enthusiasm for storytelling. But at dinner tonight, whenever he asked Luke about himself, the man had deftly deflected the subject back to Rupert.

At first Luke was full of intrigue. He acted like a man of mystery. But after a while, Rupert became frustrated at Luke's reluctance to open up about himself. He was used to one-night stands, where the sex was good and the conversation merely incidental. He was also certain Luke was giving him plenty of come-on signs. After all, the American had flirted with him even as he lay injured on his bathroom floor the night before. Rupert was more than happy to respond and reciprocate. But was it really leading anywhere? Rupert drained his wineglass and headed for the kitchen. He needed to find out.

"Can I help?" he asked. He stood in the doorway of the tiny galley kitchen.

"I'm nearly done," responded Luke. He finished wiping down the worktop with a cloth and looked at the wineglass in Rupert's hand. "Do you need a refill?"

Rupert shook his head. "Thanks, but I've had enough alcohol for one evening." He set the wineglass on the counter. "Now it's time for you to fulfill your side of the deal."

Luke put down his cloth, leaned back against the worktop, and rested his hands on the counter on either side.

"I've done the clearing up, and I've offered you my spare bed." Luke tilted his head and raised an eyebrow. "What more are you expecting?"

Rupert stepped back into the hallway and gestured with his hand toward the living room.

"Your paintings," he said. "You promised to 'take me upstairs' after supper. I've been looking forward to it."

Luke laughed and followed Rupert into the hallway. He turned to face him, and the two men gazed at each other.

Rupert leaned toward the American's kiss-shaped lips. Immediately, Luke responded by leaning away. He gently placed his hands on Rupert's shoulders and held him still.

"Whoa, boy," said Luke. "Baby steps, huh? I told you, I'm complicated. Don't want to muddle things between us. At least not while you're staying here."

Luke dropped his arms, pushed past Rupert, and began to walk down the corridor. "Follow me," he said over his shoulder. "Everything's laid out weird in this place."

At the end of the hallway, he stopped by an open door on the left and turned to Rupert. "You see, to get up to the studio, you have to go through my bedroom."

Luke entered the room and switched on a pair of glass-domed wall lights on either side of the king-sized bed. The bedroom was well proportioned and uncluttered, with simple, Shaker-style furniture. Rupert stood on the threshold and watched as the American crossed to the other side of the room. Luke bent to pick up a short wooden pole with a hook on the end of it. He raised it to the trapdoor above his head and struggled to insert the hook into a small metal loop on the hatch. With a grunt of satisfaction, he pulled down on the pole and swung open the trapdoor to reveal a lightweight metal ladder. He gave the end of the ladder a tug, and it extended with a clatter down to the floor. Luke dropped the pole, put his foot on the first rung of the ladder, and turned to Rupert.

"It's a bit of a mess up there I'm afraid," he said. "I don't usually show my work to anyone. It's kinda private."

He climbed the ladder and disappeared into the black hole of the hatchway. A moment later, the darkness was replaced with a flood of white light. Luke called through the opening. "Come on up, Rupert. But watch your step on the ladder. It's a little shaky."

Rupert entered the bedroom, walked around the end of the bed, and paused by a tall wooden dresser positioned below a large round mirror. He took a moment to look at the few items arranged neatly on top of the dresser. There was a brass carriage clock, its white face faded and streaked with brown rust stains. Leaning against it were several postcards of Dali paintings. On the left was a carefully positioned group of toiletries, and on the right was a battered old teddy bear, propped up against the wall at the back of the dresser. The bear had lost an ear, and large patches of its fur were missing.

Luke's head appeared through the hatchway.

"Ah," he said. "I see you've met Archibald. He protects me from curious Englishmen. Come on up here, and I'll show you what I waste my time on." And he disappeared again.

Rupert climbed the narrow metal ladder to the makeshift studio in the loft space of the old Edwardian house. At the top of the ladder, he stepped onto white wooden floorboards, stood up straight, and looked around him. The studio must have been about twenty-five feet long, with ample head height in the middle of the room. On either side, the ceiling followed the roofline and sloped down to the eaves of the house. The studio space was lit by five panels of white LED lights, suspended along the length of the ceiling. They were set between six large skylights, through which Rupert could see the night sky.

"Well," he said. "I never knew this existed."

Luke stood at the far end of the studio by a giant easel on which was propped a canvas about five feet high and seven feet across. Beside him, ranged along the length of the back wall, was a paint-spattered wooden table covered with a jumble of painting paraphernalia. Brushes, tubes of paint, palettes, jars of liquid, and an open toolbox littered its surface. Leaning against the low, sloping walls of the studio on either side were smaller canvases, similar in size to the ones Rupert had seen in Luke's hallway earlier. Like those paintings, these were dark, brooding works, created with angry brushstrokes. Three of the small canvases were starkly different from the others. Against a backdrop of dark, swirling clouds, they featured white oblong panels, within which Rupert thought he could see the dim outlines of heads with vague facial features.

"Welcome to my sanctuary," said Luke. "This is where I escape from the real world and create my own."

"It's impressive," said Rupert. He walked the length of the studio to reach Luke's side and turned to look at the huge canvas on the easel. Luke had barely started on this new, larger work. He had sketched charcoal outlines across the surface of the white canvas stretched tight on its frame. Rupert struggled to understand the image the charcoal marks intended to convey. They seemed to outline the upper torso of a person; whether it was a man or a woman was impossible to determine. The person seemed contorted in a strange position. The upper part was larger and dominated the canvas. Rupert studied the outline for several minutes before he commented.

"It seems very different to the other work you've done," he began. "Is it going to be a figurative piece?"

Luke's voice was excited, like a young child proudly showing off his schoolwork. "I've wanted to do one for some time, but I've never had the courage. Until now, all my work has come from inside my head. It's what I see in my mind. In my memory. The smaller canvases—the seven up here and the two downstairs—are a composite piece. Actually, the gallery over at Battersea is going to exhibit it next spring."

"I'm impressed," said Rupert. "Have you exhibited before?"

Luke shrugged. "Who knows? So I'm real nervous about this, and I'd much prefer not to."

"Why don't you want to exhibit your work?" asked Rupert.

Luke turned to the table beside him and began to create order from its disarray. He collected a handful of the paint tubes and lined them up in exact rows along the back edge of the table.

"I never intended to paint for an audience. Just for myself," he began. "I suppose it started as my therapy. It kinda helped root out some of my demons."

He placed the last of the paint tubes in the line and looked up from the table.

"That sounds pretty lame, I guess. I mean, I don't think I'm any good or anything—"

"You're going to have an exhibition," said Rupert. He turned away from Luke to look at the seven canvases ranged along the sloping wall of the studio. "London galleries don't just take anybody." He walked across to the paintings and squatted down to inspect them closely.

"Hey, wait," said Luke. "They're not placed as they should be." He picked up a large sketchpad from the table, carried it across to Rupert, and squatted alongside. He flipped over several sheets of the heavy cartridge paper until he came to a page with pencil sketches of nine rectangular panels on it.

"Here's the layout," said Luke. He showed the page to Rupert. "There's a progression to them. From chaos to order. You're not really going to get the effect while they're just leaning here, but"— he pointed to the middle panel of the group—"this is the last in the series. It represents harmony."

Rupert sat back from the panel. He was no expert in art, even after several visits to London's Tate Gallery during a brief affair with the BBC's handsome arts correspondent. But as he stared at this particular canvas, he believed he could appreciate the emotion the artist was trying to convey. The intricate brushwork generated an overwhelming sense of harmony and peace. It was painted in oils, applied thickly to the canvas. Rupert rapidly scanned the image. His eyes flicked back and forth until they rested on its central area and slowly defocused. He felt his muscles relax, and a sense of overwhelming calm settled on him.

"What is it, Rupert?"

Luke had sat down, and Rupert was aware the American was staring at him closely. The canvas was almost hypnotic in the sense of well-being it created within him. After a long pause, Rupert turned his head to gaze at Luke.

"That's quite something," he began. "The others downstairs. They were different. It's difficult to believe they were painted by the same—"

"I know," said Luke, leaning in closer to Rupert. "Put those out of your mind. Tell me about this one. It's affected you. I can tell. Describe what you feel."

Rupert looked back at the canvas. Once again, the sense of calm engulfed him.

"I can only compare it to how I feel when I go back home," he began. "There's a place where I walk in the Chiltern Hills. I found it years ago. I go there to escape my parents. There's a viewpoint I climb up to. It's difficult to find, so there's never anyone around. And when I get up there, I see the lush green of the valley laid out before me. There's no sound apart from the calls of the red kites flying overhead and the wind blowing in my face—"

Luke leaned forward and kissed Rupert gently on the cheek. Rupert turned to see Luke's deep brown eyes glisten as they stared at him with a penetrating intensity. Rupert raised a hand and placed it on the back of the American's head. He pulled him close, and their lips embraced. Timidly at first. Then, emboldened by the sensuousness of the moment, the two men fell back on the studio floor and hungrily explored each other's mouths with their tongues. Rupert traced the firm curve of Luke's chest and tight waist as he slowly moved his hand down to the inside of Luke's thighs. Luke groaned in appreciation when Rupert massaged him through the fabric of his jeans before he reached for Luke's belt buckle.

The shrill, insistent tone of a mobile phone rang out. Rupert ignored it, but it persisted. With a curse, Rupert rolled to one side, sat up, and reached into his back pocket.

"Yes, what?" he said. He held the oversized smartphone to his ear and listened with mounting irritation.

"It's all in my notes," he said at last. "Didn't you read them?"

The voice at the other end was equally agitated.

"Okay," said Rupert with a sigh. "Send the image through now, and I'll confirm the identity. But I'm damn sure it's all in the camera shot list."

He hung up the phone and looked across at Luke, who was lying back on the floor with his eyes closed, an arm resting on his forehead.

"I'm sorry," said Rupert. "It's work. There's a last-minute rush on an edit of a piece I shot in a refugee camp in Greece last month. It won't take a moment."

Luke opened his eyes slowly and sat up.

The phone beeped, and Rupert tapped the screen. An image appeared on it. Luke leapt to his feet and backed away toward the open loft hatch. His eyes were wide with terror.

"Hey," said Rupert. He stood up with the phone clutched in his hand. "Are you okay?"

But Luke had disappeared down the ladder.

CHAPTER 7

RUPERT STOOD at the top of the open hatchway, unsure what to do next. He looked again at the image on the screen of his phone. It showed the face of a Syrian man he had interviewed through an interpreter at a refugee camp on the Greek island of Chios last month.

Had Luke ever met this man? And if so, how? As far as Rupert knew, Luke had never been to Syria, and the chances of him traveling to a crowded refugee camp were remote. So what was it that had so clearly terrified the American? And it was obvious Luke had been terrified. Rupert decided he should wait a few minutes before he followed him down the ladder. To fill the time, he made a call to Sandra.

"'Ello, darlin'. 'Ow far 'ave you got on wiv 'im?"

"Look, I can't really speak at the moment. But I've got a question to ask. Why is Craig editing my refugee piece? He's just called me with some damn-fool question. I thought you were supposed to be doing it?"

There was a sigh at the end of the phone.

"This afternoon old iron knickers said the cut wasn't tight enough and asked me to lose a few bits out of the edit." There was a pause before Sandra continued. "I suppose I told 'er where she could stick it."

"Sandra," said Rupert in exasperation. "Why didn't you tell me? You know what Craig's like—"

"Yeah, about six years old and a right little know-it-all. 'Ow do you think I feel? She's done it deliberately."

"Yes, well you shouldn't have insulted her in the first place," replied Rupert, frustrated by her childishness. "I'm going to have to go in now, before he wrecks it—"

"But it's gone ten o'clock," said Sandra. "What about yer date? You can't leave 'im. He must be champin' at the bit for you—"

"It's not quite like that," interrupted Rupert. "Look, any chance you could come in too? I'm going to need you to back me up—"

"You must be fuckin' jokin', Rupert Pendley-Evans!"

Rupert held the phone away from his ear as Sandra's deafening reply hit his eardrum. He tentatively placed the phone back against the side of his head.

"If you come in, I'll tell you what happened this evening," he began.

"You can do that tomorrow," Sandra replied briskly.

"I'm out on a research trip tomorrow," said Rupert. It was almost true. In the morning he was meeting an old university friend for lunch who happened to work for the National Crime Agency. But Sandra was not to know that.

There was a long pause at the other end of the call. Rupert gambled on Sandra's desperate curiosity. He knew her too well.

"You gettin' a taxi?" she asked finally. "'Cause if you are, you can fuckin' well send one for me too."

WHEN RUPERT climbed back down the metal ladder to Luke's bedroom, he found the American sitting on the edge of his bed. His shoulders were slumped, and he stared absently at the battered old teddy bear on the dresser at the foot of his bed.

"You okay?" asked Rupert. He held the side of the ladder, with his foot on the bottom rung.

Luke lifted his head to look at Rupert. He straightened his back and stood.

"Yeah, I'm fine," he said and walked to the doorway. "Why don't I show you your room so you can get some rest?"

Rupert shook his head. "Yes, well, I'm afraid I've got to go back into work. Look, I can sleep at mine tonight. It's really not—"

"No."

Luke turned to look at Rupert.

"I'm sorry about all that upstairs. I've got a problem with… that is to say…." Luke coughed and stared at the floor. The room was still. Rupert clung to the side of the ladder and waited for Luke to explain more about his abrupt exit from the studio. Finally, the American looked up.

"I'm sorry," he said again. "There's stuff I need to tell you. But not tonight. Look. I'll get you a towel and show you your room and give you the spare key. You already know your way around the kitchen if you need to get something later."

Rupert still hesitated. His foot rocked back and forth on the rung of the ladder.

"Don't judge me." Luke almost whispered the words. "Not yet anyhow."

Rupert let go of the ladder. He crossed the bedroom to Luke and rested a comforting arm on his shoulder.

"I'm not going to judge you," he said. "I'm the last one to sit in judgment. I just don't want to upset you." He pointed to the open hatchway that led to the studio. "And I certainly did tonight. But, in your own time."

Luke turned his head and kissed the hand that rested on his shoulder. "You're a good man, Mr. Pendley-Evans. Thank you for being patient."

He slid away from Rupert's arm. "Your room's here. Right across the hall. I'll go get you a towel and a spare key."

THE VAST newsroom was busy when Rupert arrived. There was a low hubbub of chatter from the one hundred or more journalists, producers, and other staff who worked on the BBC's domestic and world news services for television, radio, and online. The ten o'clock television bulletin for BBC1 had just finished. The shiny glass-and-chrome news set was ranged along the far wall of the newsroom. An array of television lamps, suspended from the ceiling, flooded it with light. The newsreader that night was a close friend of Rupert's.

Rupert had worked with Beverly Daniels when they were both stationed in the BBC's Washington bureau. He loved her quick wit and admired her ability to keep calm amid the politically charged madness of the American capital. She was Rupert's producer for six months. When the news editor sent him to Canada to cover the election of the new, sexy prime minster, Beverly remained behind to report on the political reactions to the multiple shootings at a community college in Oregon. It was the first time she had appeared on camera. From the start, it was clear the camera loved her. In his Ottawa hotel room, Rupert had watched a recording of Beverly's first broadcast. He was certain a new star was in the making.

He headed for the editing suites on the opposite side of the newsroom.

"Rupert," called Beverly. "What are you doing here tonight? Another Royal tip-off?"

He turned and walked back toward the smoked-glass lectern in the middle of the news set. Beverly stood at the lectern and closed the lid of her laptop computer.

"Beverly darling." Rupert kissed her on both cheeks. The musky scent of her perfume filled his nostrils. "When are the American networks going to snap you up? Surely it's only a matter of time."

She laughed and rested a hand on his forearm.

"I couldn't be disloyal to Auntie BBC, now could I?" she said and tilted her head. Her long black hair fell across one side of her face. She brushed it away coquettishly with her hand. "And anyway, I couldn't leave colleagues like you behind." She looked around conspiratorially and leaned in to speak in a low voice in Rupert's ear. "But if I were to be involved in discussions with a major international network—and that's not to say I am—but if I were, would you come with me?"

Rupert looked at her and raised an eyebrow. This was hot news. If Beverly was about to be poached from the BBC's ten o'clock news, it would leave a tempting vacancy to be filled.

"What would I do?" he asked finally. "Carry your bags?"

Beverly looked around her again before she continued in a whisper.

"CNN is launching a new investigative show this winter. No one knows about it yet. They're looking for two anchors with British accents. Interested?"

"Where's it based?"

"Atlanta," Beverly whispered into his ear. "But with a passport to the world. They want the anchors to be seen at the heart of the news story. We could be anywhere. From Moscow to Manila."

"We?" repeated Rupert. He leaned back to look at Beverly. "You seem to have got this all planned remarkably quickly."

"Oh come on, Rupert." There was a hint of irritation in Beverly's voice. "I know you're as ambitious as me. Neither of us have family or partners to tie us down here. We're free agents." She leaned in to his ear again, seductive rather than conspiratorial this time. Once more the musky allure of her perfume wafted over him. "CNN saw us onscreen together in that election special. They know we're hot. The papers were full of our 'sexual chemistry.'"

Rupert was tempted. A transfer to CNN would give him a worldwide audience, with a major boost in pay. His fame in the UK suddenly felt insignificant and parochial. But his ego was bruised by the fact CNN had approached Beverly first.

"I'm not sure I could face going back to the States," he said finally. "I got burnt there last time. London's my home, and I get to travel with the BBC. Anyway. If you go, perhaps they'll give me the ten o'clock news."

Beverly turned back to her laptop.

"You don't fool me, Rupert Pendley-Evans," she said with a smile. "I'll tell them you're interested." She picked up the laptop and walked away from the set.

Rupert was about to head for the editing suites when a hand grabbed his arm.

"Oi!" said Sandra. "No need to run off like that. What did Bombshell Beverly want?"

Rupert looked down at the diminutive picture editor at his side. "Oh, we were just catching up," he replied dismissively. "Thanks for coming, Sandra. I really appreciate your help. Let's go and see what kind of a pig's ear Craig has made of the edit."

"Not so fast, mister," said Sandra. She stood in front of him and barred his way. "'Is shift doesn't finish until six tomorrow mornin', so we've got plenty of time. Before we go any further, you've got your side of the bargain to deliver. What 'appened tonight?"

Rupert sighed. "Do you want a coffee? I'm not going to talk about it in the middle of the newsroom. And I'm certainly not going to talk about it in front of Craig. Shall we go down to get some of that disgusting brown liquid from the coffee machine?"

"Ooh, you know 'ow to treat a girl well, don't ya?" Sandra rested her chin on the backs of her hands and fluttered her eyelashes at Rupert. "I'll have a hot chocolate if you're buyin'." She flashed Rupert a wicked grin. "Then I can 'ave it whipped."

Rupert laughed. They crossed the newsroom to a small area furnished with high-top tables and barstools. The dimly lit space was fitted with a microwave and a couple of vending machines dispensing hot drinks, snacks, and meals to reheat in the microwave. In the far corner, plastic cups and discarded food wrappers overflowed onto the floor from a flip-top bin. The tabletops were grubby and coffee stained. The small kitchen area was deserted. Sandra struggled up onto one of the barstools, and Rupert got a hot chocolate for her and a black coffee for himself.

"Why do they 'ave to make these bloody stools so 'igh?" complained Sandra. Her short legs dangled in midair as she tried to get comfortable in her seat. "They didn't think about bleedin' midgets like me when they built this place, did they?" She picked up the plastic cup of hot chocolate and quickly set it down on the tabletop again.

"Shit, that's fuckin' 'ot," she said and shook her scalded fingers. "Now, Mr. Pendley-Evans. What 'ave you been up to tonight?"

Rupert gave her a selective summary of the evening's events at Luke's, culminating in the American's rapid exit from his art studio.

Sandra shook her head and cautiously tried to sip from her plastic cup of hot chocolate. "Do you think 'e's a nutter? Maybe the crack on the 'ead when 'e fell over in the bathroom 'as done 'is brain in. Whose picture was it you was lookin' at?"

"Anas Ahmad, the guy who'd lost his wife and children when their boat capsized off Chios," replied Rupert. He took out his phone and showed Sandra the photograph. "Craig sent it to me to do a name check."

"And you say 'e just ran off?" asked Sandra.

"It was like something out of Hamlet. As if he'd seen his father's ghost," replied Rupert. He put the phone back in the pocket of his leather jacket, picked up the coffee cup in front of him, and took a sip.

"Damn, I see what you mean," he said as the scalding liquid touched his lips. He set the coffee cup down on the table again. "And no, I don't think it's right to call him a nutter. Or to call anyone else a nutter for that matter," he added, with a disapproving look at Sandra. "But something's disturbing him, and I'd like to know what it is."

"Why is it all the gorgeous men are bonkers, eh?" asked Sandra, oblivious to Rupert's criticism of her clumsy euphemism for Luke's mental health. She looked up at Rupert. "Come to that, why is it all the gorgeous ones are gay?"

IT WAS half an hour after midnight when Rupert arrived back in Luke's apartment. He eased the front door shut to avoid making a noise and walked gingerly down the corridor of his temporary home to the spare room. At the end of the hallway, he stopped. The door to Luke's bedroom was partly open, and he could see the American's long, muscular legs stretched out on top of the bedclothes. In the background he heard the rhythmic hum of a rotary fan, forlornly battling the oppressive heat of the close July night.

Rupert stood motionless outside the doorway. The door was open maybe six or eight inches and allowed a partial, teasing view of Luke's naked sleeping form. Rupert could see the backs of Luke's calves curve up to the indentations behind his knee joints. The taut hamstring muscles of his thighs twitched intermittently, as though he were running an imaginary race. Rupert recalled the previous night in Luke's bathroom, when he'd cradled the injured man in his arms. He remembered watching admiringly as Luke's toned muscles contracted and relaxed with involuntary spasms of apparent cold and fear. Standing here, on the threshold of the American's bedroom, temptation overcame Rupert, and he pushed gently on the door to open it a little more.

The hinges creaked as the door swung open to reveal the sharply defined curves of Luke's upper torso. The American stirred and rolled over onto his front, his arms spread across the pillows. The dark shadows of his buttocks clenched as he stretched his left leg and bent his right into a commanding sprawl across the diagonal of the bed. Rupert held his breath. Not daring to move. Not wanting to disturb this peaceful and erotic moment.

After nearly a minute, Luke had made no further movement, save for the steady rise and fall of his broad shoulders. Rupert exhaled quietly. He stepped back from the open doorway and retreated to the bedroom behind him. Tonight it was best he let sleeping Americans lie.

CHAPTER 8

RUPERT LEANED over the edge of the bed, picked up his mobile phone from the floor, and peered at the time. It was nearly nine o'clock. He cursed, dropped the phone on the floor, and lay back on the pillow. With all the distractions of last night, he had forgotten to set the alarm. At least the meeting with Jerry was not until eleven. Jerry was his analyst friend at the National Crime Agency. He had called Rupert at the start of the week, suggesting they meet for something to eat. That usually meant a tip-off.

Before then, Rupert had to make a start on the mess in his apartment. He also had to book builders for the repairs and call the insurance company. He groaned. There were three groups of people he loathed in life: accountants, property agents, and insurance salesmen. As far as he was concerned, none of them added value or beauty to the world.

Plus, if his alarm had gone off, he could have spent some time with Luke.

From the end of the corridor, he heard a quiet click as the front door closed.

"Luke?"

Rupert sat up, swung his legs over the side of the bed, and stood up. Naked, he walked across to the window and opened the heavy velvet curtains. Sunshine flooded into the room. Rupert squinted his eyelids shut. He reopened them slowly to accustom himself to the brightness of the morning. The view from the window came into focus, and he saw he was not alone. About fifty feet away was a modern, low-rise apartment block. A young man wearing sweatpants and a towel around his neck stood on a balcony of the building almost directly opposite. He raised a glass of orange juice in salute.

"Hey, Rupert," he called. "I thought your place was on the ground floor?"

It was Rupert's gym buddy, James.

"Going up in the world, are you?" continued James. "I can see something definitely is."

Rupert glanced down at the subject of James's last comment. His penis was partially erect. Rupert clumsily tried to arrange his hands in front of him to protect his modesty before he raised them in the air with a shrug of defeat.

"Morning, James," he called back. "I'm sure you've seen it all before."

James laughed.

"What are you doing there?" he asked. "Moved in with the sexy new man upstairs? That didn't take you long."

"Kind of," replied Rupert. "His bath overflowed and flooded my apartment. So he's let me move up here temporarily until my place is fixed."

"Temporarily?" repeated James, and took another drink from his glass. "That's something I do believe when it's Rupert Pendley-Evans saying those words. A man never known for his long-term relationships."

James glanced down to the small paved area below them.

"But I'd suggest you cover up before the paparazzi get wise to you standing naked at the window of your 'temporary' new home. You don't want to be front-page fodder. Again."

Rupert laughed. He made an elaborate, courtly bow to his gym buddy, moved back from the window, and crossed the bedroom floor to his open suitcase. He rummaged around for a pair of shorts, pulled them on, and stood.

"Luke?"

He walked over to the bedroom door and stepped into the corridor.

There was no reply. He called again and headed for the kitchen. On the worktop by the stove, there was a yellow sticky bearing a scrawled note.

Help yourself to breakfast. I'm not back until about four today. I'll cook supper for 7:30. Hope you can make it. Luke XOXO

Damn, thought Rupert. He would have to wait until the evening to question Luke about his actions of the night before.

AFTER A long hot shower, Rupert wrapped a towel around his waist and padded to the kitchen to fix coffee. By the side of a very sophisticated espresso maker, Rupert found another yellow sticky addressed to him, with concise instructions on how to use the machine.

> *Switch on. Wait two minutes. Put the cup under. Press start. TOUCH NOTHING ELSE. XOXO*

At least Luke had said it with kisses and hugs.

The coffee was good. Rupert carried his cup to the sitting room and stood at the window overlooking the tree-lined residential street. The rich taste of the coffee was in sharp contrast to the scalding muddy liquid he had discarded in the newsroom last night.

There was little activity in the street that morning. The office workers had already long gone to their cramped cubicles in the City. There was no sign of the residents left behind on that sunny day. The driver of a delivery truck impatiently negotiated the parked cars that narrowed the street, seeking to shave two minutes off his journey through London's traffic jams. A squirrel caught Rupert's attention. He watched, fascinated, as it climbed a mature oak tree directly in front of the window. The squirrel stopped and eyed Rupert with wary disdain for several minutes before it scampered to a higher branch and disappeared from view.

Rupert craned his head forward and peered up into the tree, seeking a better view of the animal's activity. But the large, rich green leaves of the oak tree offered the squirrel perfect cover from its observer. Disappointed, Rupert looked down into the street again.

Which was when he saw the man.

He was probably in his late thirties, dressed in a dark suit and black brogues. He stood at the entrance gate to number 54 Paton Road. As Rupert watched, the man glanced around him, lifted the latch of the gate, and pushed it open. He paused and looked up directly at the window where Rupert stood.

They held each other's gaze for several seconds before the man pulled the gate shut, dropped the latch, and walked away briskly down the street.

Rupert wished he had brought his phone into the living room to take a photo of this potential intruder. There were no CCTV cameras outside the building to record the event. Rupert set his coffee cup on a nearby bookcase and walked to the bedroom. He picked up his phone from the floor and rapidly made a note of all the details about the man's appearance he could remember.

He was black, of slim build, probably about six feet tall, although that was difficult to judge from Rupert's high vantage point. His short, curly hair was well-groomed, and he was clean-shaven. The man was good-looking and had a square-set jaw and high cheekbones. Beneath the dark jacket, Rupert had seen a white shirt with a crimson red tie.

Rupert finished his notes and read them back. They probably described any number of men he could see on the streets of London most days of the week. If one of the apartments was burgled in the next week or so, there was nothing particularly distinctive he could pass on to the police about this potential suspect.

He sighed and flicked through the list of contacts on his phone. It was time to steel himself for the call to the insurance company.

THE OFFICE building for the National Crime Agency where Jerry worked was a ten-minute walk from Paton Road. In recent years, the Vauxhall area of London had become a hub for government crime agencies. Down the road from the NCA were the headquarters of the UK's secret intelligent service, MI6. Half a mile across the River Thames was the headquarters for domestic intelligence, MI5. And now the Americans had relocated their embassy building from Grosvenor Square in the heart of the West End, to Nine Elms, half a mile from Rupert's home. Rupert sometimes wondered if there were more spies per square yard around his home than in a dozen James Bond films.

The Black Dog pub on Vauxhall Walk was already busy when Rupert walked through its doors that morning. Like so many pubs around London, the Black Dog had been gentrified to survive the fall in traditional pub trade, especially when the ban on smoking was introduced. It no longer served warm beer and preservative-packed meat pies. There was now an excellent wine list and a first-class kitchen. Rupert looked forward to an early brunch with Jerry and to find out what juicy tip-off he had for him.

"Rupert," called a voice. "Over here."

A nervous-looking man, who appeared to be much older than Rupert, half stood and gave a tentative wave in Rupert's direction. He sat at a small table tucked in the back corner of the pub, with a pint of beer, already partly drunk, in his hand.

Rupert squeezed past the tables crammed into the narrow space and walked toward Jerry.

"Hey," he said, eyeing the pint in the man's hand. "Bit early for drinking, isn't it?"

Jerry put the beer back on the table and gave an embarrassed laugh.

"Oh, you know me, Rupert," said Jerry. "Always ready for a pint. Anyway, I'm not working today."

He stretched out his arms awkwardly, and the two men embraced. Rupert felt Jerry give him a small, affectionate kiss on his neck.

"Did you come all the way from Windsor just for a chat?" asked Rupert. He pulled out a chair and sat opposite Jerry. "I would have made it another day if I'd known. I suggested we meet here because I thought you'd be at your offices down the street."

"Don't worry," replied Jerry. "Patrick and I are doing some early Christmas shopping. Then tonight we're going to see a new play at the National. What are you drinking?"

"Early Christmas shopping!" Rupert laughed. "It's July, Jerry. After all these years, you never fail to amaze me with your forward planning. How is Patrick anyway?"

Jerry took a drink from his glass and set it down in front of him.

"Not so good," he replied, after a long pause. "He's not able to use his legs well. It's a new development."

Rupert reached out a hand and rested it on Jerry's arm. "Shit, I'm so sorry Jerry. I thought they said he'd plateaued?"

Jerry avoided Rupert's concerned look and stared down at the table. "Yes, well, you know. Multiple sclerosis is a shitty thing. It makes you believe it's done its worst, then it fucks you up a bit more." He looked up at Rupert. "That's why we're Christmas shopping. At least Patrick can still walk at the moment. He might not be able to in six months' time."

Rupert rubbed Jerry's arm gently, and the two men fell silent for a moment.

"I remember how he was when you first met him," said Rupert.

"You mean the day after the college porter found me and you in your bed together?" said Jerry, with a grin.

"The abomination of Keble College, Oxford," said Rupert with a laugh. "That's how the Master described me when he summoned me to his study. I don't understand how you got off so lightly. I nearly got sent down."

"It was because it was your bed," replied Jerry. "You were clearly the seducer. I was an innocent young man of nineteen, distracted from my studies of abstract algebra and special relativity by an older and more experienced sinful student."

"Older by two months," said Rupert in mock protest. "My God. That was thirteen years ago. Where does the time go?" He pointed to Jerry's drink.

"Come on," he said. "I'll buy you this one. What will it be?"

Jerry shook his head. "One pint's enough for me this morning. I can't be drunk when I see Patrick later. Why don't we have something to eat like we planned? I'll have a coffee with it."

Rupert reached inside his jacket for his wallet. "Fine. But I'm paying. I presume you wanted to see me to give me a tip-off? That's the only reason you call me these days."

Jerry raised a hand in protest. "Hey, that's not fair. You know how it is with Patrick. He doesn't like me being away from him for more than a few hours. He's never dealt with this bloody disease very well. These days, if anything, he's getting needier than ever."

Rupert stood and laid a hand on Jerry's shoulder. "I'm sorry. I didn't mean to be so clumsy. And I'm really grateful for your tip-offs. Look. I'll go and order the food, and then we can chat."

Rupert went to the bar and ordered two full English breakfasts and a pot of coffee. When he got back to the table, Jerry was reading a copy of the *Metro*. He folded back the pages of an article and showed it to Rupert.

"Did you see this?"

Rupert took the newspaper and glanced at the story. He had read it online earlier that morning.

"The student who hanged himself in the boathouse up the river at Chiswick?" He handed the paper back to Jerry. "I was going to look into it today. They've asked me to investigate the Manwatch report on the increase in suicides among young men."

"Good," replied Jerry. "You should. There've been three similar deaths to that one in the last few months around the UK. One in a small town in Scotland, one down in the South West, and one in Northern Ireland. Each time, a man under thirty years old is found hanged. Apparent suicide."

"Apparent? Are you saying they weren't?"

Jerry leaned in toward Rupert and rested his elbows on the table. "There were a number of similarities in each case. There's enough of a pattern for me to believe there's a link between them all. You know I spend my days looking for patterns? Coordinating the reports from our ridiculously fragmented regional police forces."

"You're the UK's FBI," said Rupert, nodding.

"I do hate the media using that phrase when they describe us." Jerry sounded irritated. "We have to be very careful not to tread on the delicate toes of our regional crime-fighting colleagues. When you label us in that way, you only make them more wary."

"I stand corrected," said Rupert with contrition. Jerry was much more on edge than when they last met. Perhaps it was the worry about his husband's declining health. Rupert considered how he could give Jerry some support, but he knew it would only cause more problems. Patrick had always been fiercely jealous of Jerry's friendship with Rupert. It was more than friendship. It was the remnant of an infatuation left over from student days.

"So what's the link?" asked Rupert. "A serial killer?"

"Maybe," replied Jerry. "But if it is, he or she likes traveling. The victims are a long way from each other. The other possibility is a crime ring of some kind."

"Is there a motive?"

Jerry leaned in to Rupert. "Possibly a hate crime. All the men were probably gay."

"Are there any other similarities in the cases?"

Jerry took a small memory stick from his pocket and slid it across the table to Rupert. "Several. It's all on here." He looked up at Rupert. "Same rules as ever. Don't duplicate anything. Don't give it to anyone else. No attribution."

Rupert took the sliver of black plastic and shoved it in his pocket.

"Why this one, Jerry?" he asked. "You're sticking your neck out a hell of a long way. You usually only do that for something meaty, like a major fraud or pedophile ring."

"Why do you think?" asked Jerry. "Three gay men, possibly four now, are found dead in the space of a few months. Each killed the same way. Each with strange religious icons on them—"

Rupert looked up. Jerry had caught his attention.

"It's all on the memory stick," Jerry continued. "And our chums in the regional forces aren't interested." He reached forward and gripped Rupert's arm. "However equal the law now makes us, the reality is, outside the metropolitan areas, they still don't give a damn."

CHAPTER 9

THE VICTORIA Line train rattled noisily through the Tube tunnel deep under Green Park and on to Oxford Circus. The carriage was packed with summer tourists. Rupert and Jerry clung to the grab bar above their heads. They were squeezed between a group of Italian students from a language school and four businessmen shouting an earnest conversation about profit margins to each other. Rupert had planned to pick up a rental bike after he and Jerry had finished brunch. He hated the confines of the Tube. But when he learned Jerry was going to Oxford Street for early Christmas shopping with his husband, he offered to join him on the journey. As they crammed into the train at Vauxhall station, he instantly regretted the decision. The Victoria Line was notorious for being one of the most overheated lines in summer.

The train screeched to a halt at Oxford Circus, and the doors clattered open. Passengers surged onto the platform, and Rupert and Jerry were carried along by a wave of sweaty humanity. Up the stairs and onto the escalator.

Rupert pulled out his phone. He stared at the screen and waited for the internet connection to kick in.

"Every time," said Rupert. "I swear I'm not going to do that again. Every time, I forget how packed the Tube is these days."

"Why do you think we live in Windsor?" Jerry stood behind him on the crowded escalator. "I have a comfortable journey on the overground train. Straight into Vauxhall in the morning, with no overheated Tube travel."

"But Windsor's so boring," said Rupert. His phone regained its internet connection and chirruped several times. A message from Grindr flashed on the screen. "I really don't know why you and Patrick moved out of London."

"Because we don't need 'the scene' like you do," replied Jerry. "When are you going to stop clubbing every night? And sitting on Grindr every waking hour? Aren't you getting a little old for that?"

Rupert turned on the escalator step to glare at Jerry.

"Me, old?" he said. "Isn't it you getting old? Living in leafy Windsor with your husband, your two Yorkshire terriers, and your rose garden? Don't marry me off just yet. There's life in this old dog yet."

They reached the top of the escalator. Rupert, still facing backward, stumbled off. Jerry reached forward and grabbed him. They stood to one side and let the sea of people push past to the ticket gates. Jerry kept his hold on Rupert.

"You know I care about you, Mr. Pendley-Evans," he said. "That's why I worry about you so much. You flit from one fuck to the next. We're not at Oxford any longer. Those student days are long gone."

Jerry sniffed and blinked his eyes. He released his grasp and rubbed at an imaginary mark on Rupert's leather jacket.

"Now," continued Jerry. "I'm off to get tinsel and a new fairy for the top of the Christmas tree."

He leaned forward and kissed Rupert lingeringly on the lips. "Take care, my abomination of Keble College." And Jerry disappeared into the crowd.

Rupert stood for a moment and watched the seemingly endless flood of people shove past him. He was unprepared for Jerry's critical commentary on his lifestyle. He knew his college friend had always had a soft spot for him. When he thought about it, that was probably why Jerry continued to feed him information from the NCA, at considerable risk to himself. But the comments had stung Rupert more than he would have expected. For the first time in a while, his self-assured confidence ebbed away.

Rupert fumbled for his Oyster card and headed for the ticket barrier. He was not going into the office straightaway. He had an errand to run first.

THE BELL above the door at Daunt Books in Marylebone High Street announced Rupert's arrival. It was a place he came to often. The bookshop was a brisk ten-minute walk from the BBC headquarters in Portland Place. Rupert had spent many happy hours dawdling among its well-stocked shelves. After El Ateneo in Buenos Aires, he considered it the best bookshop in the world. Rupert walked to the back of the shop to the art section. He was looking for a book about England he was certain would be perfect for Luke. A thank-you gift for his hospitality while Rupert's apartment was being fixed up.

Rupert ran his fingers lovingly along the spines of the books on the shelves, in search of his quarry. On the lowest shelf, he found it. *Ghastly Good Taste*, by former English poet laureate the late John Betjeman. Rupert's own copy was battered and dog-eared. He had thumbed through it a thousand times or more since Jerry presented it to him thirteen years ago. Betjeman was one of Rupert's heroes. A poet, a writer, an architectural campaigner, and a nostalgic for an England long gone. Plus, he had been a brilliant broadcaster. Rupert hoped Luke would like *Ghastly Good Taste*. It was about the England of Miss Marple and Lord Peter Wimsey. Rupert knew it was probably vastly oversentimental of him, but it had been an impulse he could not resist. He hoped Luke would enjoy the book as much as he did.

RUPERT HURRIED through the narrow side streets from the bookshop back to the BBC. It was after two, and he was going to be late for his editorial meeting with Eileen Jones. She would want to know what he had found out, and he had yet to look through the contents of the memory stick Jerry gave him that morning. He also wanted to make a call to a pathologist friend, who might know more about the Chiswick suicide.

He emerged into Harley Street, the home of London's expensive private doctors and consultants. He waited for the traffic on the busy street to clear. About a hundred yards down, on the opposite side, he saw the tall, toned figure of Luke. His temporary roommate stood on the steps of a distinctive Georgian building, in front of a large, black door. Rupert shouted and waved, but his voice was lost amid the noise of a high-sided truck crawling past. By the time the truck moved on, Luke was no longer visible.

Rupert crossed the street and strode briskly down to the building. To the left of the imposing black door was a security keypad, below which was a large brass plate. Five smaller plates were fixed alongside a door buzzer. The larger plate read London Psychiatry Partners. The five smaller plates listed the names of physicians. He looked up. A camera observed him.

He heard footsteps behind and turned to see a woman wearing a navy blue trouser suit and carrying a large cardboard box. She walked up the steps behind him.

"Can I help you?" she asked.

"No, I'm fine, thanks," replied Rupert. "But do you need a hand?"

"Are you here for an appointment?" asked the woman, ignoring his question.

Rupert hesitated. Here was an opportunity to get into the building. His instinct as a journalist was to seize the moment. But he knew it was a gross invasion of Luke's privacy.

"No," he replied at last. "I've got the wrong place. Can I help you with that?"

"That's very kind," replied the woman. "Could you push the doorbell?"

Rupert did so, and the woman looked up at the camera. A moment later, there was a loud buzz from within. The woman leaned against the door and pushed it open. She turned to Rupert and gave a brisk nod of her head, then disappeared inside. The door closed behind her.

Rupert stood on the steps a moment longer. Whatever was wrong with Luke, whatever had caused his outburst last night, at least it looked like he was getting help. Rupert glanced at his watch and cursed. Now he was really late for the editorial meeting.

"I'M SO sorry, Eileen," said Rupert. "The train broke down outside Oxford Circus."

Eileen Jones sat typing at a desk in her small, glass-walled office to the side of the main newsroom. She had her back to Rupert when he opened the door, and continued to type as he waited patiently on the threshold. He knew she could see him. There was a convex mirror fixed on the wall above her desk. It allowed her to see people behind her. After several minutes, the typing stopped. Eileen closed the lid of her laptop and swiveled round in her chair.

"I don't have long," she said. "I can't imagine you've got much to tell me. It's only a day since I gave you the assignment."

Rupert remained in the doorway, waiting for an invitation to enter his editor's office. None was forthcoming.

"Not quite," he replied. "I've received some information about a series of apparent suicides around the UK in the last three months. The NCA are investigating them because of similar, suspicious circumstances. They might not be suicides."

Eileen looked over the top of her spectacles at Rupert.

"That's a crime piece," she said. "Not a societal impact story with political ramifications. That's what I commissioned from you yesterday, and I took you off the news desk for it. Sounds like you're hankering to get back to news."

"Eileen," replied Rupert, "I think it's too early to disregard the story in relation to the Manwatch report. I need to correlate the statistics."

"You say these deaths are in the last three months. The Manwatch report is for the last four years. I very much doubt some serial killer has been on the loose for that long without his efforts going unnoticed. Stick to the Manwatch report. Who have you spoken to so far?"

"Well, the NCA, as I mentioned—"

"I meant at Manwatch," Eileen cut in. She peered intently at Rupert. "You haven't even spoken to them yet, have you?"

Rupert didn't reply.

"Mr. Pendley-Evans." Eileen shook her head. "You know as well as I do what I need. Don't come back until you've got it." She turned back to her desk and glared at him in the convex mirror. "And if you haven't got it in a week, we'll sit down and review your career together."

Rupert stood in the doorway for a moment longer. *I know what you need, Eileen Jones*, he thought to himself. But he knew better than to say it out loud.

SANDRA WAS at her desk when Rupert returned. "Wotcha, darlin'," she said. "You've got a face like a wet weekend." She propelled her chair across the threadbare carpet and pulled up alongside Rupert as he sat down.

"What's in this mystery, gift-wrapped package on your desk, by the way?" She picked up the bag from the bookshop and shook it. "An' more importantly, 'oo's it for? Or can I guess?"

"I'm going to kill that woman very soon," said Rupert. He threw his notebook down on the desk. "She's trying to spike my story even before I've finished writing it."

"I thought you was all kissy-kissy wiv 'er again? Certainly seemed that way after yesterday's meetin'. She takes you off news desk and gives you a feature piece to do." Sandra leaned across and rested her head on Rupert's shoulder. "Or are you bein' Mister Precious all over again?"

Rupert pushed her away and pulled his chair toward the desk. "Go away, Sandra. I've got work to do."

"An' what happened when yer got back last night?" Sandra was not giving up. "Was 'e still up? Is your tasteful little gift in that bag sayin' 'thank yer for 'avin' me,' or 'please will yer 'ave me tonight'?"

Rupert swung round on his chair and glowered at Sandra. She responded by crossing her eyes and blowing kisses at him. Rupert continued to glare at her for several seconds before he gave a deep sigh. He stretched out his long legs, flexed his arms behind his head, and shook his head.

"I really don't know what's going on, Sandra," he said. "He gives me come-on signals. Then, when I make a move, it all comes to a shuddering halt. Normally when that happens, you won't see me for dust. But this time…."

"Ooh, Rupert's in love." Sandra jumped to her feet, clasped her hands to her heart, and flickered her eyelashes at him. He shook his head and turned back to his desk.

"Go away, will you? I really need to catch up after this morning."

Sandra picked up the bag with Luke's gift inside and dangled it in front of Rupert's face.

"Go on," she said. "What you got 'im, then? I 'ope it's somethin' sexy."

Rupert grabbed the bag away from Sandra and put it on the opposite side of the desk.

"It's a book by Sir John Betjeman if you must know," he replied as he logged into his laptop. He took out the memory card Jerry had given him earlier and plugged it into the side of the computer.

"Who the fuck's 'e when 'e's at home?" asked Sandra.

"He's a poet," replied Rupert, testily. "From the twentieth century. He was poet laureate in fact."

Sandra burst out laughing. "Poet to the Queen? Now I understand." She leaned forward to whisper in Rupert's ear, "You queens 'ave got to stick together after all, 'aven't yer?"

CHAPTER 10

RUPERT REACHED into his desk drawer and pulled out a pair of large headphones. He plugged them into his phone and chose a playlist he had long ago dubbed his "Sandra Silencer." He loved Sandra deeply, but right now she was driving him up the wall.

He turned to his laptop and gazed at the contents of the memory stick. There was only one document, and it was encrypted. Rupert entered the password Jerry had given him for any documents they exchanged.

Jerry's report was seventy-eight pages in total. The first four were a tightly written summary of four male deaths, with similarities, coincidences, and speculation highlighted. The remaining seventy-four were copies of the autopsy reports for three of the four deaths Jerry had outlined to Rupert. The report for the Chiswick death was not yet available. Rupert rapidly skimmed through the four-page summary. The Chiswick autopsy was being handled by a pathologist called Dr. Rosalind Friend. A piece of luck for Rupert. He and Rosalind had been on the planning committee of London's Gay Pride three years in a row. She was about five years older than him, with a good heart and an acid tongue.

He paused the music on his phone, dialed a number, and took off his headphones. The call only rang twice before it was answered.

"I wondered how long it would take you to call me. What do you want?"

"Lovely to speak to you too, Rosalind," replied Rupert. "Have you missed me?"

"How can I miss you?" came her response. "You're never out of the newspapers."

"You don't have to read them, my sweet," countered Rupert.

"That's true," mused Rosalind. "And the ones you're in are such rags. Aren't you embarrassed to be splashed across their pages?"

"Should I hang up and call back later?" asked Rupert. He was not in the mood for Rosalind's barbed jibes. "It's clearly a bad time."

"Oh, don't be so sensitive, young man. This is what they call banter. I'm sure you must have heard it before. Although maybe your little fawning, sycophantic entourage in the BBC is far too deferential to subject you to that." Rupert heard Rosalind take a long drag on a cigarette. She exhaled as she spoke. "Think on this as an education for your eventual ejection into the real world."

Rupert was about to reply when she pressed on.

"But to the matter in hand. I presume you're calling me about twenty-year-old Richard Barnett. Found hanging in a Chiswick boathouse three days ago. Death by strangulation. Traces of a drug, apparently a refined derivative of scopolamine, in his bloodstream and urine. No other signs of violence or injury to the body. Healthy young man in a reasonable physical condition. Bizarre religious paraphernalia concealed in an inner pocket of the boy's—sorry, young man's—jacket and hidden in his shoes." She exhaled noisily before continuing. "You can't come round today because I'm too busy, but if you want to visit tomorrow, I expect at least a bouquet of roses for my troubles."

Rosalind's explosive laugh turned into a fit of coughing.

"You know those things will kill you, don't you?" said Rupert.

"No, Rupert," replied Rosalind, inhaling deeply on her cigarette. "Ridiculous deadlines with no extra resources from my so-called superiors will kill me. Cancer sticks will simply make that experience more bearable."

"Red or pink?"

"What?"

"The roses," replied Rupert. "Red to match your eyes or pink to go with your pouting lips?"

Rosalind laughed. "That's better. See what ten minutes with me does for you? How's your love life by the way? Still with that Portuguese boy with a big dick and no brain?"

Rupert had to think for a moment.

"Oh, you mean Antonio," he replied, as he recalled the three-month fling he had started back in April. "He was from Brazil, not Portugal. That was ages ago. We went to Berlin together, and he never came back. He's moved in with some Nordic god he met in a leather bar."

"Oh, you boys and your obsessions with dressing up," said Rosalind with a sniff. "Women are far more straightforward."

Rupert laughed loudly. The sound drew a quizzical look from Sandra.

"Now I know you've been drinking the formaldehyde again, Rosalind," he said. "How is Alison, by the way? It would be good to have another night out with you two again."

"Only if we go to a place where you're not distracted by some twink after less than an hour," said Rosalind. "Now, I have to go. I've left a death by drowning out of the chiller for over half an hour, and he's beginning to whiff a bit. See you at two tomorrow with a dozen red roses."

And she hung up.

Rupert sat and stared into the distance. Rosalind's question about his love life brought his thoughts back to Luke. He closed his eyes and recalled the sight of the sleeping American from the previous night. He pictured the slope of Luke's broad shoulders, and the steady rise and fall of his chest. The light from the half-open doorway had highlighted curls of black hair down his abdomen, on his upper arms, and on the exposed thigh of his right leg. Rupert felt a stirring in his groin. He held his eyes closed and indulged the memory of a moment unfulfilled. The moment when he could have crossed the threshold to enter Luke's room. Rupert slowly ran his hand down the top of his thigh and imagined it belonged to Luke.

"Oy, sleepyhead!"

Sandra's voice cut through his daydream. He opened his eyes and shook his head.

"I'm going to get coffee. Do you want it black?"

RUPERT COULD hear an Adele album playing loudly even before he opened the front door of Luke's apartment that evening. As he walked down the hallway toward the kitchen, the music switched to a track by an American artist he had listened to when he lived in Washington. Rupert could hear Luke singing along loudly. Rupert's calls of greeting went unheeded. He stood in the kitchen doorway and admired the sight of Luke's swaying hips. They described a slow arc to the rhythm of the singer's ballad.

"At last I've found what I'm looking for," sang Luke loudly. "This is the love I've longed for—"

Luke expertly crushed garlic and salt using the flat face of a sharp knife. Within a minute it had transformed into garlic paste. He picked up the chopping board and scraped the paste into a skillet of hot butter. With a loud sizzling noise, the rich smell of frying garlic hit Rupert's nostrils.

"I can sing it out loud, but words are not enough," Luke continued singing. He put down the chopping board and turned, the knife still in his hand. He froze when he saw Rupert watching him.

"Oh my God. How long have you been standing there?"

"Long enough," Rupert said with a laugh. "Please, carry on. It's a sight for sore eyes after today."

Luke turned back to the stove. "I can't perform with an audience." His voice was subdued. "I can't sing anyway."

Rupert stepped into the kitchen and placed the bookshop bag on the worktop to the right of Luke. He turned and put an arm across Luke's shoulders.

"I disagree. You have a great voice. And your hips move even better."

Luke twisted his shoulders awkwardly. He reached away from Rupert and retrieved a bunch of parsley, which he rapidly chopped and scraped into the skillet of frying garlic. Then he reached for a bowl of uncooked king prawns and stood, bowl in hand, stirring the garlic and parsley with a wooden spatula. Rupert dropped his arm from Luke's shoulder and picked up the bookshop bag. He pulled out the gift-wrapped book and offered it to Luke.

"I didn't mean to embarrass you, Luke," he said. "Here. I got this today. A small thank-you for putting up with me."

Luke put down the spatula and the bowl of prawns. He wiped his hands on the black-and-white striped apron he was wearing and took the gift from Rupert.

"Oh, that's real kind," he said. "But you shouldn't have."

He looked at Rupert for a moment, as though uncertain what to do next. Finally, he leaned forward and kissed Rupert slowly on the lips. Rupert blinked his eyes shut as their lips touched. He wanted to experience nothing but the smell, taste, and touch of the American. Luke bore the scent of shower gel and the comforting taste of home cooking. His lips were full and soft as they pressed gently against Rupert's. For an instant, they parted slightly, and Rupert allowed his own to open. He let his tongue venture forward. It connected with Luke's, and their lips opened farther. They explored each other's mouths, tentatively at first, but with increasing urgency.

Rupert reached up and placed both hands on the back of Luke's neck. He held the American's head firm as he continued his satisfying exploration of Luke's mouth, of his tongue, of his lips. Luke's hands pressed on Rupert's hips and slid down in a slow massage to rest finally on Rupert's buttocks. Confident he had been given permission to take the American, he reached down to grab the stiffening cock in Luke's crotch.

"Hey, hey." Luke pulled his groin away and raised his hands to push firmly on Rupert's shoulders to restrain him.

Rupert breathed deeply and stared at Luke. He was puzzled. The American raised an eyebrow and tilted his head. "We're not playing a scene in a porn film, Rupert."

Luke lowered his eyes to Rupert's hand as it swung close to his crotch. He looked up and gazed intently into Rupert's eyes. "I'm a real human being here. We didn't meet in some dark room at the back of a sex club. If you want that, I'm afraid you've got the wrong guy."

Rupert leaned back against the worktop, hands to either side of him. He took a deep breath, exhaled slowly, and straightened up.

"I'm sorry," he began. "It's just, I thought—"

Luke rested the flat of his hand on Rupert's chest and pressed gently.

"I'm not looking for a quick fuck, Rupert," he said. "That's not me. You're a seriously beautiful man. Certainly on the outside. And I really want to get to know if you're a beautiful man in here." He patted Rupert's chest gently with the palm of his hand. "But it's better we don't rush things. Trust me. You need to know—"

Luke was interrupted by the sound of the smoke alarm's sudden, insistent beeping. He turned to the skillet on the stove. The garlic and parsley had turned almost black, and smoke poured into the kitchen.

"Oh shit," he said and turned to Rupert.

"Are you okay with charcoal garlic king prawns?"

THE EVENING was sultry and still once more. Luke had moved the rotary fan from his bedroom and installed it in the dining room. It swept a cooling breeze back and forth in a slow, undulating rhythm. The fan brought regular yet intermittent respite from the stifling heat for the two men who sat at the small dining table. Luke thumbed through the pages of the book Rupert had given him.

"This is so neat, Rupert," he said. "This guy Betjeman writes about the British Victorian architecture I love. How did you know? When I need inspiration, I go walk along Cromwell Road to look at the Natural History Museum, or up to the Royal Albert Hall. This guy likes the same stuff I do. And he pokes fun at all the modern shit you guys built in the '50s and '60s."

Rupert set down his knife and fork and licked his lips appreciatively.

"Those prawns were a triumph," he said. "No trace of burnt garlic whatsoever." He started to clear away the plates. "Yes. Britain's got a lot to thank Betjeman for. For a start he saved its architectural heritage. After the war they wanted to knock it all down and begin again. They thought everything had to be modern. Betjeman campaigned against the government of the day destroying some of our major architectural treasures. He's a big hero of mine."

"Well, he's definitely a hero of mine too," said Luke. He set the book on the table and extended his hand to Rupert. "Gimme those, and I'll go get the main course. It's ribs and grits."

"Grits?" queried Rupert. "I've heard of them but never had them before. What exactly are they?"

Luke took the empty plates from Rupert and stood up. "Ground corn. And you're in for a treat. 'Cause I make them taste real good."

He disappeared into the kitchen and returned a few moments later with two plates piled high with ribs and grits.

"There's more when you're through with that," he said and set a plate in front of Rupert.

"Hey, looks like my diet just flew out the window again," said Rupert, eyeing the mound of food on his plate. He looked across at Luke, who sat opposite. "I'll have to live at the gym for the rest of this week now."

"What are you complaining about?" asked Luke. "Grits are great for your digestion, low in calories, and rich in vitamins, minerals, and proteins. It's only when you add cheese and butter and shit they become fattening. And I stripped all the fat I could find off the ribs." He leaned forward and winked. "I was only thinking of that well-honed body of yours when I put this meal together."

Rupert raised his glass of water and saluted Luke. "I applaud the chef for tonight." He took a drink from his glass and set it down on the table. "So. It's your turn to tell me about you." Rupert picked up his fork and looked at Luke. "You had the start of my life story last night. Over to you."

"But I've already told you," said Luke. "I can't remember. I can't remember any of my life before I came to London."

"What is it? Amnesia?"

"Kind of."

"You mean you can't remember anything? Where were you before London?"

Luke sighed. He set down the rib he was about to eat and wiped his hands on his napkin. "The first thing I remember about London is waking up in a police cell. I've no idea how I got there. Apparently I walked into the police station in Battersea, and told them I didn't know who I was."

"What happened?"

"I was there for hours."

"Shit, Luke," said Rupert, putting down his fork. "How did you get out?"

"I have no idea."

Luke picked up a rib from his plate and took a large bite. Rupert watched as he slowly chewed and finally swallowed. There was a silence as he stared off into the distance.

"But you did get out?" asked Rupert when he could wait no longer.

"Oh yes. The next day. Somebody turned up with my wallet, proof of my identity, and a mobile phone with a few names and numbers in it. I didn't know any of them. It was freaky."

"Who was it?"

Luke drank from his glass of water. "That's the weird thing. He didn't hang around, so I never met him. It seems I've been living in Britain for nearly two years, studying art."

"But you only moved into this place a few months ago," said Rupert. "It was while I was in Yemen. I'd always meant to come and say hi. But somehow I didn't have the time. That was—"

"Six months ago," replied Luke. "The afternoon of February twenty-third. A Tuesday. I've got all the rental documents to prove it. The problem is, I don't remember any of it."

Rupert gestured to the ceiling with his fork. "What about your paintings up in the studio? When did you start on those?"

"The composite?" asked Luke. "Oh, pretty well straightaway."

"But if you couldn't remember anything, how did you know you could paint?"

Luke shrugged. "I just knew. The materials were there the day I arrived in this apartment. I started sketching that evening."

Rupert picked up a rib from his plate and began to gnaw at it. "So the amnesia. What can you do about it? Is that why you're seeing a psychiatrist?"

Luke's hands froze, a barbecued rib halfway to his mouth.

"I'm not," he said.

"But I meant to say before," said Rupert. "I saw you in Harley Street earlier today. You were going into that London Psychiatry place—"

Luke dropped the rib on his plate with a clatter. "What are you? A spy?" His eyes widened, and his nostrils flared. He stood up and knocked his chair over. "Are you checking up on me?"

"No, no." Rupert was shocked by Luke's sudden change of mood. "It was after I bought you the book. I was walking back to the BBC through Harley Street—"

Rupert's phone rang loudly. He pulled it from his pocket and saw there was a video call from Sandra. He looked at Luke.

"I'm really sorry, it's someone from the newsroom—"

Luke was backing away from the table, his eyes wide and staring. He turned, stumbled over his fallen chair, and almost ran down the corridor. A moment later, Rupert heard the front door slam.

CHAPTER 11

RUPERT DROPPED the phone on the table and slumped back in his chair.

"Are you there? Hello?" Sandra's voice cut through the stillness of the room. She was shouting above background noise from what sounded like a busy club. Her voice dropped, as though speaking to someone with her.

"I don't know. All I can see is the bleedin' ceilin'. I'll 'ang up and try again."

The phone went dead. Rupert sat up straight in his chair and picked up the phone. A few moments later, it rang again. He answered the call, and after a few seconds, Sandra's face reappeared on the screen.

"There you are," she said. "What 'appened to you? We're down the RVT. It's lip-sync night. We thought you two might like a bit of fun. Ty's goin' to be struttin' 'is stuff to Gloria later, so I—"

"Luke's cooked supper," Rupert interrupted. "I told you this afternoon." He was not in the mood to hear anything about Sandra's antics at the RVT, or Royal Vauxhall Tavern, the gay club fifteen minutes down the road from his apartment.

"Yeah, I know. But after you've eaten," replied Sandra. "Anyway. It would be a chance for you to show 'im a few of yer dance moves. Then 'e might think you're a good mover in—"

"He's not here." Rupert interrupted the torrent of words once more. "He's gone out."

"What? You mean 'e's gone to get somethin' for the meal?" asked Sandra. "Look. Why don't you both come down after you've finished eatin'? We'll 'ave got goin' by then anyway, so you'll—"

"No, Sandra," Rupert interrupted her a third time. "He did that thing again. When you called just now. The phone seemed to set him off."

"Sorry love, it's deafenin' in 'ere. I can't 'ear yer," said Sandra. "Whatever. Come after you've eaten. If you two don't come, then we'll just assume yer shaggin', and we'll be dead envious."

Sandra's image froze on the screen before it disappeared altogether. Rupert threw the phone on the table and looked around the dining room. He wished he had some idea of where Luke had run off to, or even if he would be coming back tonight. But apart from the psychiatric clinic in Harley Street, he had no idea where Luke would go. The romantic evening had started so promisingly. Now it was a mess, and Rupert was not sure what he felt.

He stood up. Complicated. It was getting complicated. And Rupert did not do complicated. He picked up the plates with their half-eaten food on them and headed for the kitchen. Rupert made a decision. He would clear away, get his jacket, and go to the Royal Vauxhall Tavern to join Sandra. It was a while since he had seen her hunky housemate, Ty, an American who worked as a flight attendant with Virgin Atlantic. He was a boisterous bear of a man, and Rupert had shared a bed with him once before. Maybe meeting Ty tonight would be compensation for the disastrous evening. If Rupert saw Luke along the way, he was not sure what he would do. He hoped he would not need to make that decision tonight. He remembered watching Ty perform his Gloria Gaynor act at the RVT once before, and it brought the house down. Perhaps it was just what he needed.

THE ROYAL Vauxhall Tavern was on the corner of a busy road junction on the south side of the River Thames, fifteen minutes' walk from the apartment. Its proximity had been a deciding factor when Rupert had chosen to move to Vauxhall eighteen months ago. Since his early twenties, he had been a regular at the RVT, London's oldest gay venue. He loved its relaxed atmosphere and its rich history. In the eighties, the RVT was a regular haunt for Freddie Mercury and many other stars. There was even a story that Freddie Mercury had smuggled Princess Diana into the bar one night, heavily disguised with a beard and Muir cap. But above all, the Royal Vauxhall Tavern was a safe haven for the bizarre in London. People who came to the RVT were not desperate to be fashionable, as in so many other London bars. Instead, they had their own unique style, and at the Royal Vauxhall Tavern, no one questioned it.

As Rupert pulled open one of the anonymous heavy doors that night, a wall of sound assaulted his ears. He pushed his way into the Tavern's crowded bar. Most people had their backs to him, facing the small stage at the far end. The lip-sync show had already started. A large bear of a man was on stage, belting out his own, very individual lip-sync performance of Beyoncé's "Single Ladies." He wore a large silver wig and had glitter liberally sprinkled in his enormous bushy beard. He wore a black Lycra wrestling suit, trimmed with white feathers, black net stockings, and what must have been size 13 black stilettos. At each rendition of the chorus, he turned to an equally bearlike man who stood in the front row. The spectator was wearing leather jeans, a white T-shirt, and a leather waistcoat. The singer bent down and gestured to his ring finger. The grinning bear in the audience blew kisses in return.

Rupert looked over the heads of the crowd to search for the diminutive Sandra. He turned to scan the few tables ranged around the outer wall of the bar and spotted her in the far corner, sitting with Ty and a girlfriend whose face was vaguely familiar. Sandra waved frantically, and Rupert eased his way through the crowd, away from the stage and toward the table.

"Where is 'e, then?" shouted Sandra above the thumping beat of Beyoncé. "I've been tellin' these two all about yer latest conquest. You know Ty, dontcha? And you remember Donna? She's moved to CNN's London office now."

Rupert remembered he had met Donna once before, when Sandra and Ty had given a much-delayed Halloween party in the spring. A very drunken Ty had thrown himself at Rupert for much of the evening, seeking another night of passion. But Rupert was turned off by the state Ty was in and had spent much of the party trying to avoid him. Eventually Ty proposed his undying love to Rupert in front of everyone and then threw up. Donna and Sandra came to Rupert's rescue, helped him to clean up Ty and put him to bed. Rupert remembered Donna had said she was a graphics designer in another part of the BBC.

Rupert leaned across the table, and kissed Donna on either cheek. Ty stood, shoved his chair away, and wrapped his bearlike arms around Rupert's neck.

"Hello, you gorgeous man," said Ty. "How can I begin to say sorry for what happened back in April? I've been hanging my head in shame ever since."

Rupert doubted that very much. Ty was one of life's rubber balls; he kept bouncing right back. Rupert found it very appealing.

"Forget it," he said. "I'm looking forward to hearing you let rip with your Gloria Gaynor later. Where's your frock?"

Ty tapped the side of his nose and gave a knowing wink. "A surprise. I'm changing in a while. Can I get you a drink? It's my round."

"Thanks, but I'm off the alcohol tonight. I'll have a Beck's Blue, thanks."

"Sure," replied Ty. "Be right back. Then I want to hear all about your new guy."

"He's not 'my new guy,'" protested Rupert. He looked across at Sandra.

"What have you been saying?" he asked. Sandra pouted. Rupert turned back to Ty. "It's all lies you know. Never trust a word out of her mouth."

Ty laughed and went off to the bar. Rupert sat down next to Sandra.

"Don't I get a kiss, then, lover boy?" she asked.

Rupert leaned across and kissed her on either cheek.

"If you've told them anything I told you in confidence," he said into her ear, "I'll kill you, Sandra Giles."

She put her hand on his thigh and squeezed. "You know I wouldn't do that, Rupert baby. An' I know there's somethin' wrong tonight. Why don't you tell me all about it?"

"Sure. But I'll be quick before Ty comes back," replied Rupert into her ear. "First, you've got to swear to me you haven't said anything to him. Or to Donna especially. I don't want it all over CNN's newsroom tomorrow."

"What do you take me for? I just told them you were fuckin' the brains out of a gorgeous mystery American."

Rupert glared at Sandra furiously.

"Joke, Rupert," she said and squeezed his thigh again. "You know I wouldn't say anything." She dropped her voice and added, "Especially now that Donna works for the evil empire. Lighten up, will yer?"

She turned to look at Rupert.

"So, tell Aunty Sandra what's 'appened."

Rupert briefly described the events of that evening.

Sandra picked up her glass and drained her drink. "So 'e's a good kisser," she said. "It's a start. What else does 'e do for you?"

Rupert sighed. He was uncertain how to begin. He had only known Luke a couple of days, but the man had already got to him in a way he had never felt before. Except maybe once. But that was many years ago, when he was younger and more naïve. In the intervening years, Rupert had experienced several relationships, and he liked to think that each one was a development on the previous. That he had learned from his mistakes each time. Except this time, he was not sure what mistake he was making.

"It's not like that, Sandra," he replied. "To be honest, I'm not sure what it's like. He's got a great body, he's a great kisser, and I really wanted to jump into bed with him this evening. But when he stopped me, it was kind of okay. I was happy to go along with it. I really didn't expect that. But I just feel good in his company." He sighed. "But when he behaves like this, I don't know where the hell I am."

"So you reckon you're just mates, then?" she asked. "You're not even goin' to be fuck buddies?"

"I don't know," replied Rupert, shrugging. "Maybe. And maybe more than that. Anyway. I'm not sure I want a long-term relationship in London at the moment. Maybe I should back away now, especially as he's so bloody complicated."

"You seem to be givin' in a bit easily," said Sandra. "You've 'ardly given the poor bloke a chance. Anyway, you're not attached. You've got a fabulous apartment. Well, you will 'ave, once you get yer ceilin' fixed. And you've got a great job in London, even if you 'ave got old iron knickers breathin' down yer neck all the time."

"Well...." Rupert paused for a moment before he continued, "I can't say too much just now. But I might not be staying around London in the future. So it wouldn't be a good idea to start anything right now."

Sandra looked at him suspiciously.

"Where are you off to, then? Shit, that wasn't why you went 'ome last weekend, is it? You're not goin' back to live with Mummy and Daddy, are yer?"

Rupert laughed. "That's the last thing I'd ever do. I don't think my lifestyle would be to everyone's taste in Middle Claydon."

He looked around the crowd that filled the Royal Vauxhall Tavern that night. He could see Ty standing at the bar, flirting shamelessly with the fit young barman. As if sensing Rupert's gaze, Ty turned and looked in their direction. He waved and blew Rupert a kiss. He was a very good-looking man, Rupert thought. Just not so good at controlling his alcohol intake. Nevertheless, he might prove to be Rupert's compensation for the evening.

Sandra kissed Rupert on the cheek. "Don't go too far away from London, will yer, love? 'Cause I'll miss yer like crazy." She looked across at Donna on the far side of the table and gave her a wave. Then she whispered in Rupert's ear, "And if you take one of them anchor jobs in Atlanta with CNN that Donna's been talkin' about, I'll kill yer. Now. Go and 'elp Ty carry the drinks. 'E's gaggin' to get 'is 'ands on yer again."

Rupert stood up and pushed his way through the crowd to the bar where Ty was standing. He wondered how much Sandra's friend Donna knew about the presenter jobs at CNN. He also wondered if she knew he was being approached about it. So much for Beverly Daniels's claim that she had a big secret and no one else knew. If it was already common knowledge, maybe he should give Beverly the nod that he was interested in the move to Atlanta. But that depended on whether he wanted to move out of London and try working in the States again. Especially after what had happened last time.

He reached the bar just as Ty turned and handed him a bottle of Beck's nonalcoholic beer and a rum and Coke.

"That's for you and Sandra," said Ty. "I'll bring the rest."

Rupert turned to head back for the table, but Ty put an arm around his waist and pulled him back to the bar.

"Just a second," said Ty. "I wanna check you're really okay about what happened at the party. I felt such an ass that night. Seriously." Ty rested his hand on Rupert's chest and stared intently into his eyes. "I just want you to know I think you're a really great guy, and I don't want to screw up anything between us. You know we're Sandra's best gay friends. She's told me you're seeing some really cute American guy, and I'm totally cool—"

"He lives upstairs, and I met him two nights ago," Rupert interrupted. He was really going to have to have a word with Sandra about her mouth. He looked at Ty's worried, puppy-dog eyes. He noticed how much the American had got himself into shape in recent months. He was wearing a white ribbed T-shirt, which highlighted his toned figure in all the right places.

"I'm not seeing him at all," continued Rupert. "Luke's just putting me up temporarily while my apartment gets fixed." He put the bottle of beer and Sandra's drink down on the bar counter next to him. He leaned forward and kissed Ty on the lips. A pleasant, musky aroma of beard oil wafted in his direction. Their lips parted, and Rupert's beard enmeshed satisfyingly with the American's. As Ty's tongue surged forward to explore, Rupert got a strong taste of dark beer. Ty slipped his hand down from Rupert's waist and reached around to stroke his thigh.

"Not at the bar, please."

The voice came from behind them. The two men separated reluctantly and looked back. The fit young barman wagged a finger in mock admonishment.

"I've got customers to serve," he said, by way of explanation.

Ty leaned across the bar. Before the young man had a chance to avoid him, Ty kissed him full on the lips.

"And you do it so beautifully, honey," he said. He picked up his glass of beer and a second glass of rum and Coke from the counter.

"Come on, Rupert," said Ty. "Let's go give the ladies their drinks."

Ty headed back to the table. Rupert had started to pick up his bottle of beer and Sandra's glass of rum and Coke when his phone vibrated in his pocket. He took it out and looked to see who was calling. It was Luke.

CHAPTER 12

RUPERT BREATHED deeply and answered the call. Before he could say anything, Luke began to speak.

"Hey, Rupert, I'm real sorry. Look. Come back now. I'll tell you everything, I promise."

Rupert leaned heavily against the bar and opened his eyes. He saw Ty had returned to their table with the drinks. He turned to look for Rupert, waved, and blew a kiss. Rupert decided his life had a habit of offering tempting forks in the road at completely the wrong moments.

"Really?" he said into the phone. "That's what you promised tonight at supper. But you didn't get very far. You even accused me of spying on you—"

"I know, I know," replied Luke. "I was a complete jerk, and you have every reason to be angry with me. You've got to understand. I'm a real mess at the moment. I didn't need to warn you, because it's so damn obvious. Look, we've only just met. But what I said in the kitchen is true. You're a beautiful man, and I really want us to get to know each other. But only if that's what you want. I don't want to frighten you off. So, let me tell you everything I know. Then you can choose to walk away from this head case—"

"No, no," interrupted Rupert. "Just. Hang on a minute." He paused to gather his thoughts. He had followed one golden rule in his adult life. Never take on the waifs and strays of the world. They held him back and threatened to pin him down with emotional baggage. It was Christoph, his first lover, who had taught him that golden rule. Rupert remembered the irony of what happened following the advice. Christoph ended the relationship. Abruptly. After twelve months. Rupert wondered what Christoph was doing now.

"Hey Rupert? Are you still there?"

"Yes, I'm here. I'm actually at the Royal Vauxhall Tavern with some friends. They invited me down after you left. They've just bought me a drink."

"I'm sorry."

The two men said nothing. Rupert was frustrated by the way events had gone. But he was surprised to find he felt no anger toward Luke. Instead, he was curious to know more about the man's mysterious memory loss. Above all, he wanted to spend more time with him.

"I'll make my apologies and come back," he said finally.

SANDRA WAS not convinced by Rupert's excuse. She stood next to him and gripped his arm.

"Why do they need yer to review the second refugee piece tonight?" she asked, looking at him suspiciously. "They're not usin' it until next week's show. You've got bags of time."

"There's been a development in Greece," he replied. "And they may run it sooner on *BBC World* if I update it tonight."

It could easily be true, he thought. There were always developments in the long-running story of the exodus of refugees from continental Africa to Europe.

"But I thought you wanted to air it first on the national news?" said Sandra. "Oh, wait a minute. Is this 'cause you're thinkin' of—"

Rupert nudged her hard, and she stopped midsentence before she could blurt out anything indiscreet about the CNN job.

"Oh, sorry, darlin'," she said with a wink. "Mum's the word, eh?"

"You're going to miss my starring moment," said Ty, pouting at Rupert. "I was about to go get my frock on."

"Sandra can video it on her phone for me," replied Rupert. "Can't you, love?"

Ty stood and leaned across the table to Rupert.

"I hope I'm going to see you again soon." He kissed Rupert on either cheek. "I was looking forward to catching up. I'm off to New York tomorrow."

"Give me a call when you're back," replied Rupert. "I promise to buy you a drink. Sorry I didn't have time for the one you bought me tonight."

Rupert was about to leave when Sandra tugged hard on his arm. He bent down, and she whispered in his ear. "Beware men pullin' strings, Rupert love. Don't let 'em become yer puppet master."

RUPERT CLOSED the door of Luke's apartment behind him and stood in the entrance hall. He pulled his mobile phone out of his pocket, made sure it was switched to silent, and put it on the narrow hall table.

"Hey, you were quick."

Luke stepped out of the kitchen into the hallway. He was stripped to the waist. "I was clearing things away and spilled barbecue sauce all over my T-shirt." He held up the garment to show a dark stain down its front. "I'm just going to get a new one."

Rupert stood for a moment and admired Luke's partially naked form. The hall lights reflected on his ebony chest. They highlighted a scattered line of curly black hair that extended from between the curves of his pectoral muscles to the waistline of his jeans. Rupert gazed for a moment at the shape of Luke's toned, well-developed upper body. He felt a swell of desire surge through him. Rupert slipped off his leather jacket and dropped it to the floor.

"You better soak that T-shirt in water right now," he said. "Otherwise you may as well throw it away."

He walked down the hallway to Luke. "Don't bother to put on another," he continued. "You look good just as you are."

Luke held out his hands with their palms facing toward Rupert. "I'm real sorry for what happened earlier. I need to finish telling you—"

Rupert leaned forward and silenced him with a kiss on his lips. "Later." He stared into the deep brown portals of Luke's eyes. "Let's just enjoy the moment together now."

Luke started to speak, and Rupert kissed him once more. "And I promise," he continued, "I won't turn this into a porn film. You're right. I have a habit of rushing at people like a bull in a china shop. You set the pace. I'm prepared to wait and take it easy. You know I find you a very attractive man."

Luke leaned forward and slid his tongue slowly around the edge of Rupert's lips. "So are you, beautiful Englishman." He took Rupert's hand and intertwined their fingers. "Thank you for coming back tonight. I didn't think you would."

Luke led Rupert down the hallway to his bedroom and stopped by the open doorway. "I'll be right back. I'm just going to try saving this T-shirt from death by barbecue sauce."

Luke gently pushed Rupert across the threshold. He walked back down the corridor, and Rupert heard the water run in the bathroom. He sat on the edge of the bed and looked around him. He had a strange sense of naivety, not dissimilar to his first night with Christoph. His impatient lust for Luke was tempered by an adolescent nervousness.

Rupert stood up and walked to the tall wooden dresser at the foot of the bed. Luke's battered old teddy bear, Archibald, caught his attention. Nestled in the bear's lap was a faded photograph. Rupert picked up the photo. It showed six people, their faces fuzzy, not quite in focus. They were standing in a dramatic cityscape, with mountains in the background. It looked like a family gathering. There were a man and a woman in the middle, hand in hand. Ranged on either side of them were two boys and two girls. The children were of varying ages. The youngest looked about ten. One of the boys could have been almost twenty.

"I found that in my portfolio case yesterday."

Rupert turned to see Luke standing in the doorway. He had removed his jeans and was wearing a simple pair of black briefs.

"I've no idea how it got there," Luke continued. "It certainly wasn't in the portfolio case the day before, when I brought it back from the gallery."

He walked across the bedroom and stood next to Rupert. "Another mystery for us to solve." He took the photograph from Rupert's hand and put it back in Archibald's lap. "Later."

Luke turned and tugged Rupert's shirt from the waistband of his chinos. Slowly, he teased the shirt upward. Rupert raised his arms, and Luke slipped the shirt off and let it drop to the floor. He paused, his arms resting on Rupert's shoulders, his eyes fixed on Rupert's face.

When the two men embraced, it was explosive. Fierce. Their hands and tongues explored each other's tense, expectant bodies. Rupert slid his palm up the curve of Luke's thigh to massage his groin. This time Luke did not pull back. Instead he moaned appreciatively in response. Luke's hands fumbled with the belt on Rupert's chinos. The buckle separated, and Luke rapidly unbuttoned his fly. He reached his hand deep into Rupert's briefs and wrapped his fingers around Rupert's hardening cock. Rupert groaned with pleasure as Luke gently squeezed and relaxed his grasp.

Luke ran his tongue down the side of Rupert's neck and nestled it into the hollow of his shoulder, moistening and caressing it with a rhythmic regularity. He moved back to the depression at the base of Rupert's neck and began to descend. Rupert's cock hardened still more. When Luke's tongue reached his chest, a spasm of pleasure soared through Rupert's body. He reached down and gently squeezed Luke's firm black nipples. The American moaned deeply and briefly paused his journey of stimulation. He sighed in ecstasy before his tongue resumed its explorations. On to Rupert's navel.

Luke released his grasp of Rupert's cock and wrapped his fingers around the fabric of Rupert's briefs. As he tugged firmly, both briefs and chinos dropped to the floor. Luke allowed his tongue to slowly slide down from Rupert's navel to the base of his cock. At the same time, he brought his hands up Rupert's thighs, above his waist, over his taut stomach muscles, and finally to his chest, where he grasped Rupert's nipples between finger and thumb and massaged them firmly.

Rupert's body twitched in an uncontrolled shiver of rapture. He leaned back against the wooden dresser and looked down as Luke's tongue progressed along the shaft of his cock and tenderly caressed its head. Rupert's breathing became shallow and rapid as waves of involuntary muscles spasms took over his body.

Luke opened his mouth wide and thrust forward. The head of Rupert's cock slid over Luke's sensuous, constantly flexing tongue to press against the back of his throat. At the same time, Luke continued to work on his nipples, sending wave after wave of preorgasmic flexes through Rupert's body. Just as he grew ready to explode in a burst of erotic ecstasy, Luke pulled back. He looked up at Rupert and tilted his head. There was a flash of mischief in his eyes.

"Do you want to come now?" whispered Luke. "Or do you want to fuck me, and come inside me?"

Rupert breathed deeply. Not since Christoph had he experienced such an intense and skilled manipulation of his pleasure.

"I so want to fuck you," Rupert replied. "Do you have a condom?"

Luke leaned back against the foot of the bed. "Shit. No, I haven't." He gazed up at Rupert. "You're the first guy I've had in this apartment. At least as far as I know," he added.

Rupert laughed. "Well, I'm certain this isn't the first time you've given head. You're fucking amazing."

He bent down and hooked his hands under Luke's armpits. The American rose to his feet and pressed himself close against Rupert. He rolled his pelvis gently from side to side, rubbing his stiffened cock against Rupert's.

"I don't know what it was, but you triggered something in me," said Luke. His chest rose and fell as he breathed deeply. "I have no memory of ever doing that with a man, but it felt instinctive."

He looked deep into Rupert's eyes. His mouth inches away, his hot breath brushed across Rupert's face.

"And it felt good."

Rupert rested his forehead against Luke's and placed his hands tenderly on either side of his face.

"I've got condoms downstairs in my place," he said. "But I don't want to leave you right now. So I'll tell you what we're going to do."

Rupert leaned forward and kissed Luke, enjoying the sweet taste of his own precum on the American's lips.

"We're going to go over to the bed. And you're going to do what you did for me just then. At the same time, I'll be doing the same for you. And if we happen to come at the same moment, this evening will be anointed with the blessing of perfection."

Luke's broad chest rose and fell. He inhaled and exhaled deeply several times before he finally spoke. "And after that, my perfect Englishman, you can stay in my arms until morning." He took Rupert's hand in his and held it against his cheek. "That way, I'll finally sleep the sleep of contentment."

CHAPTER 13

RUPERT AWOKE from his doze to find Luke still nestled on his chest, his arm draped across Rupert's shoulder. The American's breathing was slow and even. Occasionally, his body twitched as it reacted to the imaginary demons of his sleep. The two men lay on top of the bedclothes, their combined body heat more than sufficient to comfort them in the stillness of the July night.

Through the window, Rupert could see a faint lightening of the sky, as the night prepared to give way to the inevitable dawn of a new day. At this time of night, there was no sound of traffic, but he could hear the occasional, insistent calls of songbirds in the trees on either side of the street outside. He guessed it was around 4:00 a.m., but he reached to the side table for his mobile phone to check. Only then did he remember he had left it in the hallway on his return to the apartment that night, not wanting a call to trigger another strange disturbance in Luke.

He repositioned his arm on the American's shoulder. Luke stirred. He stretched his long legs and unfurled his fingers to pull them tight on Rupert's shoulder. His lips parted to exhale a deep sigh. Rupert shifted his hand and cupped it around the back of Luke's head. Gently, he massaged Luke's scalp through the tight curls of his short black hair. The American's eyelashes flickered, and he opened his eyes. Rupert kissed him on the forehead.

"You okay?" asked Rupert.

Luke tipped his head in assent. The long, brown eyelashes flickered shut, and he sighed once more. "What time is it?"

"Early," replied Rupert. "Nearly dawn."

He kissed Luke and stroked the side of his head. "For a man who's lost his memory," he said in a low voice, "you certainly know how to give pleasure."

Luke chuckled and opened his eyes. He reached up and kissed Rupert on the lips. For a moment, his mouth parted, and he gently bit on Rupert's lower lip, allowing his tongue to massage behind the gentle bite of affection. "You too, Rupert."

The two men lay in silence for several minutes; their chests rose and fell in empathetic breathing. The hint of a cool breeze from the open window swept across the room. Luke shivered.

"Cold?" asked Rupert.

Luke shook his head as he lay in the hollow of Rupert's chest.

"Not with you here," he replied.

"I have to ask you," said Rupert after a few more minutes of silence. "What changed? Yesterday evening in the kitchen, you wanted to take things slowly. Then last night, when I came back here, and you were standing there without a shirt...."

"That wasn't deliberate, you know," interrupted Luke. "I genuinely tipped the goddam sauce over it. I'm damn sure I wrecked it too."

He looked up at Rupert, and his deep brown eyes sparkled. "What changed? Lots of small things. But significantly, you took care of me the night I blacked out in the bathroom. You put up with me when I flipped. Twice now. And last night when I called you, you came back. You didn't judge. And you stood there in the hallway...." His voice tailed off, the sentence left unfinished, and looked at Rupert forlornly. "I'm so lost. And so screwed up right now. I'm trying to make sense of things, and I've got no one I can trust." He looked away from Rupert as he added, "But maybe there's you."

Rupert stroked the side of Luke's head. "You know, I don't usually do waifs and strays. It's too risky for me. I was with a guy once, and he got sick. And I nursed him through pneumonia. I was really in love with him. And I thought he was in love with me. Then he got better. And he went away."

Luke shifted his arms to lay them across Rupert's broad chest. "I'm not going anywhere Rupert. At least, not as far as I know. But I don't know what's happening with my life right now."

He propped his head on the palms of his hands. "You know, caring for someone when they're sick is a part of love. But it's only a part. There are so many aspects to love. So many ways we can show it. So many ways we can feel it being shown to us." He sighed and rested his head back on Rupert's chest. "Somehow, I know I've been in love in the past. I just wish I knew it was true."

Luke gently played with the curls of hair in the hollow of Rupert's chest. Rupert laid his head on the pillow and thought back to his previous failed relationship. Andrew was a journalist working for the *Washington Post* who had recently returned from a posting to China. They met at a party, and after less than a month the two men moved into a one-bedroom apartment together in Georgetown. They were inseparable for nearly six months, working side by side for their rival employers. Andrew was rushed to hospital one night, where the pneumonia was diagnosed. When he finally left the hospital, Rupert nursed him through recovery. After four months, Andrew announced he had accepted a posting to Berlin. Rupert was furious and felt betrayed. That was eighteen months ago. He had not heard from Andrew since.

"So tell me everything you know, my little waif and stray," said Rupert. "I want to help you."

Luke raised an eyebrow at Rupert. "Don't repeat the patterns of the past. If we are to fall in love—"

Rupert started to speak, but Luke lifted his hand and covered Rupert's mouth.

"If we are to fall in love, I don't want pity. I don't want to be simply the invalid patient you care for. I'd like to think there's more to me than this fucked-up individual you see lying across your chest at the moment."

Rupert pushed Luke's hand away from his mouth and leaned forward to kiss him. "I'm sorry. I won't say waif and stray again. It's a stupid phrase." He kissed Luke once more and leaned back against the pillow. "Tell me everything you know. Maybe I can help you find out more."

"According to my driver's license, my name is Luke Diamond. I'm thirty-two years old, and I live here. I'm licensed to drive any vehicle up to seven tons and—"

Rupert laughed. "I don't need all the fine details, like your license number. Do you have a passport?"

"Oh, yes. I've got a US passport with an immigration visa in it. I found a bunch of energy bills and water bills shoved in a drawer in the kitchen. They're all in my name, and they date back six months. That must be when I moved in here. But I can only remember from February twenty-third. The day I walked into the police station."

"What about your mobile phone?" asked Rupert. "You said there were numbers in it."

"Yes, twelve of them. The landlord, the telephone company, the gallery...." Luke stopped and sat up, his eyes alight with excitement. "Hey. I forgot to say. That's a weird thing. I'm in their exhibition next spring."

"You told me yesterday," said Rupert. "Remember? When you showed me your work. It's a great achievement."

Luke dismissed the praise with a shake of his head. "Yes, but I never asked them to exhibit my work. They booked me in ages ago. They told me when they rang to confirm some details two days after the police brought me back here."

"But they must have seen you and your work at some stage," said Rupert. "Did you ask them when?"

"They said they saw my work last Christmas," replied Luke. "And they were very excited by its originality, and it would fit into a themed exhibit they're doing next spring. But I've got no memory of going to see them at all."

"Have you been back to the gallery since you spoke to them?"

"I went over there, the day after they called. But it's like, fancy. Real upscale. I chickened out and didn't go in. Instead, I came back here, picked up a paintbrush, and kept on painting. It was like, really weird. I didn't know I could paint. But I could. I just seemed to know what to do. That's happening a lot. I find I can do stuff, like cooking and—"

"Sex?" said Rupert with a smile.

Luke chuckled. "Yeah. That was my latest revelation tonight." He leaned forward and playfully flicked Rupert's nipple with his tongue. "But maybe I'm just a quick learner."

"I don't believe anyone gives head like you do on their first outing," Rupert said. "You could read me like you were plugged into my brain. You've got incredible empathy."

"But I don't remember ever doing that before," said Luke. He leaned his head forward on his hands and stared up at Rupert. His eyes were so beguiling, like a puppy waiting for his master to rub his head. "That's why I wanted to take things slowly with you. I was terrified I'd have no idea what to do. I felt like a virgin."

Luke absentmindedly combed the hairs on Rupert's chest between his fingers. "That's how my life is right now. It's like I'm doing this stuff for the first time. When in reality, I know I must have done it all before."

"I've got to ask you," said Rupert gently, "what is it about my phone? Twice now it's freaked you out. How come the same doesn't happen when your phone rings?"

"Here's the thing," began Luke, and he turned his head to look up at Rupert. "Have you noticed anything missing in this apartment?"

Rupert looked around the bedroom and pondered for a moment. There was nothing he could think of. In his mind, he tried to picture the living room. It held everything he would expect in a typical apartment.

"What business do you work in?" asked Luke.

"Television," replied Rupert. "Oh, sure. But there's quite a few people I know who don't have a TV these days. It's becoming the fashionable thing among the chattering classes. They shun the big TV in the living room. They say it's an ugly piece of furniture. They call it a symbol of passive supplication to the controlling media moguls—"

"You seriously think I'm like that?" asked Luke, his eyes widening.

"Well, I didn't mean you specifically," said Rupert hurriedly. "I just thought you'd decided not to have one. A lot of people watch TV on their laptops instead."

"I don't have one of those either," replied Luke. "Nothing electronic with a screen."

"Why?"

"Because if I see one, it terrifies me."

"But there are so many screens. All around us," said Rupert. "How do you avoid them? Shit. They even have them on the bus. There's a TV security screen in the shop on the corner—"

"I try to avoid going in there," said Luke bluntly. "I don't use the bus or the Tube. I ride a bike everywhere. I can't go into stores that sell electronic goods. Even when—"

Luke stopped. He lowered his eyes and said nothing for a moment.

"Okay, I didn't tell you the truth earlier," he said finally. "You were right. I am having therapy. That's where I was yesterday. I go to Harley Street once a week to see Dr. Jemima Ballantyne. Not that I get much out of it."

Rupert gently began to massage the back of Luke's head. "It's okay. How did you find her to book yourself in?" He stopped rubbing and sat up. "Hang on. A private psychiatrist in Harley Street? How can you afford it?"

Luke rolled off Rupert's chest and leaned over the edge of the bed. He reached out to the bedside cabinet and opened the drawer, pulled out a piece of folded paper, and handed it to Rupert.

"That was shoved in with the bills and other paperwork I found," he said.

Rupert unfolded the paper and stared at it in amazement. It was a statement from Coutts Bank in the name of Luke Diamond. The account contained over 250,000 pounds.

"Not bad for an art student who's a crazy guy, huh?" said Luke with a smile. "Stick around, kid. You just found yourself a sugar daddy."

CHAPTER 14

THE COMPUTER screen flickered into life. Rupert opened up the search engine and typed in the name *Luke Diamond*. Screen after screen of results appeared. He sat back in his chair and looked around the newsroom. It was one o'clock, and the lunchtime bulletin had started. Rupert's desk was in the far corner, out of vision of the glass-and-chrome news set surrounded by cameras. When a bulletin was on air, he made sure he could not be seen in the background of any shot. A colleague had once been caught on camera, picking his nose. The tabloid newspapers had a field day with the enlarged images from the video footage. Not that Rupert would ever pick his nose. Not in public anyway.

He turned back to his computer screen and added some key words to Luke's name: Artist. Battersea Bridge. He added Luke's age. There were still thousands of results. He sat thinking for a moment before he picked up his phone.

"Will? Hi, it's Rupert here. I was wondering if you could help me with a police report?"

Will Sutherland was a cute police officer Rupert had picked up in the Royal Vauxhall Tavern on a cold November night four years ago. They had seen each other a few times for sex, but Rupert soon found their shared enthusiasm for European cinema was stronger than any sexual chemistry between them. Periodically, they continued to meet for screenings of a Buñuel or Almodóvar season on the South Bank. It seemed to satisfy Will, and the young man's access to Niche RMS, the police database in the UK, was useful for Rupert. Sharing the confidential information was an instantly dismissible offense for Police Constable Will Sutherland, but he seemed not to care.

"Hey, Rupert," said Will. "I was just thinking of you. They're doing a bunch of Derek Jarman screenings this month. It's part of the gay cinema retrospective. Do you want to go see *Caravaggio* on the big screen?"

"Oh sure," said Rupert. "Are they showing *Sebastiane* as well? One of the sexiest films I've ever seen. Very daring for 1976. It's got an erection in it. A very beautiful one too. The first ever in a film not classified pornographic."

Will laughed.

"I'll check, but I'm sure they must be screening it. I know other pieces of trivia about *Sebastiane* too," he added, enthusiastically. "It was the first English-language film shot in Britain with English subtitles. And Jarman had the script translated—"

"Into Latin by a top scholar," interrupted Rupert. "Yes, I know. Apparently the professor was rather turned on by the more erotic bits. Find out the screening dates, and let's see if we can go see one of them. It's been a while since we last met up. Now. Any chance you can help me with this report?"

Rupert heard Will sigh deeply.

"It's getting kind of tricky you know. They're tightening up on access to the main database. But I'll see what I can do."

Rupert told Will the few details he knew about the night Luke walked into Battersea police station.

"You say he'd lost his memory?" asked Will. "I would have thought they'd have handed him over to mental health services on a section 136. That's the procedure we follow in the event that a person is a danger to themselves in a public place. Of course, they would normally need to consult a health professional before they did."

"But could you take a look?" asked Rupert, ignoring Will's passion for precision. "He's a bit of a mystery man. I can't seem to get any background on him."

"Why do you need to know?"

Rupert hesitated.

"It's probably best I don't tell you anything," he said finally. "Then there's nothing you have to deny, if you get asked."

"Hmm," replied Will. "I'm not sure why I keep doing this." He dropped his voice to a whisper. "Do you know what will happen to me if they catch me?"

"You get out of that dead-end job and go work on film festivals," replied Rupert. "Like you always wanted. I told you, I've got a contact in the British Film Institute if you ever decide to quit. Your film knowledge would be gold dust to them."

"Okay, your flattery wins me over. As ever," said Will. "I'll call you back in my break later on. And, yes," he added, "I'd like to meet your contact at the BFI. It's time I got out of here. Before I go nuts."

Rupert ended the call. He turned to the phone's photo album and found the image he had recorded before he left the apartment that morning. It was a close-up of the photograph sitting in Archibald's lap on Luke's bedroom dresser. Rupert downloaded the picture to his computer and enlarged the image to fill the screen. The faces of the six people in the photo were indistinct, even more so with the picture magnified. An older man and woman held hands in the middle of the frame. Two young women stood to the left of the couple and two young men to their right. Rupert peered closely at the young men. They could have been aged anything from sixteen to their early twenties. They wore dark suits and ties and stood erect, almost at attention.

"Is that your Luke?" asked a voice from behind him. Sandra jabbed a finger at the two boys standing on the right of the screen. She leaned in to the screen to stare closely at the image. "Certainly looks like 'im."

"Do you think so?" Rupert looked again.

"Oh yeah," Sandra said with conviction. "A lot younger. But it's the way 'e's standin'. Surely you can see it? Look at them legs. And the shape of 'is face."

Sandra swiveled around and hoisted herself up onto Rupert's desk, where she sat swinging her legs back and forth.

"Where'd you get that?" she asked.

"It was in his bedroom last night," replied Rupert. "Luke said it had just appeared—"

"In 'is bedroom, eh?" Sandra said loudly. "So 'ow was your night of passion, then?"

Rupert looked round to see if anyone had heard. He raised a finger to his lips.

"Will you keep your voice down, Sandra Giles," he said with irritation. "I don't want my private life broadcast round the entire newsroom." He turned away from her and peered again at the image on his computer screen.

"If it is him, I wonder if that's his family." He looked at the cityscape behind the group in the photograph. "It would be good to know where it was taken," he continued. "It doesn't look like anywhere I know."

"Well, 'e's got an American accent, so chances are it's somewhere in America." Sandra grinned. "That narrows it down a bit. Why don't you send it to Betty in the Washington bureau? If anyone's goin' to know it's 'er."

Betty was the fixer in the BBC's Washington offices. It was her job to make sure camera crews and correspondents got the resources they needed, wherever they were in the United States.

"Yes, good idea," said Rupert. "I'll send it over now."

"So you still 'aven't told me," said Sandra, watching Rupert draft the email on his computer. "Did the earth move?"

Rupert clicked Send, closed the lid of his laptop, and stood up.

"Can't talk now," he said with a smile. "I've got an appointment with a dead body at two o'clock. Can't keep him waiting."

THE SCREAM of a police siren and the insistent hammer of a pneumatic drill hit Rupert's ears when he walked out of the BBC's news headquarters in Upper Regent Street that lunchtime. London was packed with summer tourists, and noise was all around him. He paused at the side of the street, waiting for the traffic to clear so he could cross to the middle where the taxis waited.

"Mr. Pendley-Evans! Mr. Pendley-Evans!"

Rupert avoided looking behind to see who was calling him. From time to time, fans would stop him in the street. Usually, the attention flattered his ego. But today he was late for his meeting with

Rosalind, and he knew she would seize the opportunity to pour scorn
on his timekeeping. Rupert stared at the faces of the drivers in the
cars, willing them to stop. As he spotted a gap in the traffic, he felt a
hand on his shoulder. He turned to see a man, out of breath, standing
at his side.

"Mr. Pendley-Evans," said the man. "I need a few minutes of
your time."

"I'm sorry," said Rupert, irritated when the man continued to
rest his hand on Rupert's shoulder. "I'm late for a meeting. You can
write to me at the BBC if you want."

"It's about Luke."

Rupert turned. The man was as tall as Rupert, well-built and
smartly dressed in a dark suit and crimson tie. He spoke with an
American accent.

"What about Luke?" asked Rupert.

"Can we go for a coffee somewhere?" asked the man. "I need to
explain some things to you."

"I told you. I'm going to be late for an appointment. What
about Luke?"

The man's grasp on Rupert's shoulder tightened. "I want you to
stop seeing him. You'll damage him if you don't."

"Who the hell do you think you are?" asked Rupert angrily. He
pushed the hand from his shoulder and stared at the man as recognition
dawned. "Hey. You were at the apartment the other morning. I saw
you try to break in."

The crowd around them surged forward as the traffic cleared,
and a stream of people pushed in front of Rupert. When the wave of
bodies finally thinned, the man had gone. Rupert stood at the side
of the street for a few moments longer and scanned the sea of faces
around him. At last, irritated and confused, he looked back at the clock
on the front of Broadcasting House. Half past one. He was going to
be very late.

"I'M NOT sure I've got time for you now," said Rosalind, her back
turned to Rupert. "You never were on time. Every bloody Pride
committee meeting, you turned up half an hour late." She spun

round in her swivel chair and looked over the top of her pink half-moon glasses. "Is it an affectation, or are you just terminally rude? I can't imagine how you survive in a newsroom, surrounded by deadlines."

"Come on, Rosalind," said Rupert, breathless from his sprint up four flights of stairs in the crumbling Victorian hospital wing at the back of Fulham Town Hall. "I'm only twenty minutes—"

"Do you know how long it takes for a corpse left out of the icebox to lose vital evidence through decomposition? Twenty minutes. Do you know how long it takes for a brain to lose all chance of recovery after the heart stops beating? Half that time."

Rupert slumped into a battered high-back armchair, curiously out of place in Rosalind's cramped, shabby office.

"And I'd be careful what you're sitting on," she continued. "I dropped a spleen on that chair by accident this morning."

Rupert hurriedly lifted his freshly laundered chinos off the seat of the chair and gingerly felt around with his hand. It seemed dry enough, but through the pungent scent of formaldehyde that permeated the office, there was a distinct, ever-present smell of putrefying flesh. The carpet was threadbare and covered in suspicious-looking stains. The walls were pockmarked with holes and dents and painted a shade of green never featured on a designer's paint chart.

Rosalind reached behind her for a thin brown folder and tossed it over to Rupert.

"Here you are," she said. "It's the draft of the report and the evidence photos. I printed them off for you in case you get all squeamish on me and back out of going down to the morgue."

Rupert opened the folder, and eight large-format photographs slipped out.

"I hope you haven't had any breakfast," Rosalind added. "I know how delicate you are."

"What happened to him?" asked Rupert, breathing through his mouth to stop the smell of formaldehyde adding to his growing nausea.

"He hanged himself. I thought you knew that." She leaned forward to look at the photograph Rupert was holding. "Oh. You mean the damage? Well, he wasn't very good at it. Most suicides aren't. The beam he hanged himself from wasn't high enough. If it's a short drop, then the neck doesn't break. Death by slow strangulation. Did himself a lot of damage in between."

Rupert shoved the photographs back into the folder and dropped it on the floor next to him. He put his head between his knees as the wave of nausea threatened to engulf him. After a moment, he sat up and rested his head against the high back of the armchair.

"You've gone a funny shade of ashen," observed Rosalind. "Do you want some water? It's only a little stale."

She reached for a glass jug clouded with limescale, and a chipped china mug. Written on its side was A Corpse is for Life, Not Just for Christmas.

"Forgive the lack of bone china," she said, handing Rupert the mug. "The NHS doesn't have the same budget for luxuries as the BBC."

She turned back to her desk and pulled up a report on her computer screen.

"They're still getting confirmation on the toxicology report," continued Rosalind. "But it looks like this chap had the same drug coursing through his veins as the other ones."

"Yes, I know about the other three."

Rosalind turned to look at him with a puzzled expression.

"How?" she asked. "I only found out because of my little network of pathology chums."

"A friend of mine tipped me off," Rupert said without elaborating on the details. "He says there was one in Scotland, one in Northern Ireland, and one in the South West."

"And presumably you won't tell me who your knowledgeable source is," she said with a sniff. "Have you seen the other autopsy reports?"

Rupert's stomach was still in a turbulent condition. He kept his mouth shut and simply nodded. Breathing deeply, he hoped he would not embarrass himself in front of Rosalind.

"Well, with young Richard Barnett, that makes four dead. All by hanging. All across the country. No pattern. If it's a serial killer, then he must have a Megabus season ticket."

"The other autopsy reports mentioned some religious artifact found on the victims—"

"Ah, yes," said Rosalind. "The 'Liberated' crucifixes." She reached across her desk for a small plastic evidence bag and tossed it across to Rupert. "This one's different. I need to give it to the police when they roll up next. Found it in his underpants, of all places."

Rupert examined the object secured in the bag. It was a silver crucifix, just over an inch long. The words Liberated, VA were embossed on the crossbar.

"The other reports said they found a silver coin with Liberated First stamped on it concealed on the body," said Rupert. He took out his mobile phone and searched for Liberated, VA.

"Here we are," he said, reading from the screen. "Liberated's a right-wing university in Virginia. It's funded by the televangelist who blames us gays for the world's changing weather system."

"Nat Jefferson? Oh, he's a sweetie," said Rosalind. "He's the one who believes women shouldn't have the vote, and a husband has the right to 'take' his wife, as he quaintly puts it, whenever he wants."

Rupert took out his phone and photographed the crucifix. He looked up and raised an eyebrow at Rosalind.

"When did you say you're seeing the police next?" he asked with what he hoped was his most beguiling smile.

"Rupert Pendley-Evans. Are you suggesting I delay handing vital evidence to our brave boys in blue so you can steal a lead in your shabby little media witch hunt?"

Rupert laughed but said nothing.

"I finish at four today anyway," said Rosalind. "Well, a bit after four, now you've made me late. They probably won't get it until tomorrow afternoon."

"Thanks, Rosalind," said Rupert. He stood up and kissed her on the cheek. She pushed him away and reached across her desk for a bunch of keys.

"How's your stomach?" she asked. "There's a body in the morgue waiting to see you. I'd better get you a sick bag before we head downstairs."

CHAPTER 15

ROSALIND SLAMMED the office door behind her and turned the key.

"God knows why I lock it," she said. "It's got be someone with a pretty warped sense of pleasure who'd want to steal my collection of human anatomy souvenirs."

She led Rupert through a battered green fire door and back down the windowless stone staircase of the Victorian hospital building. Partway down the second flight of stairs, Rupert's mobile rang. He stopped on the half landing, pulled the phone from his pocket, and answered it.

"Hey, Luke," he said. "What's up?"

"There's a man here looking for you," replied Luke. "He's from the insurance company."

"Oh shit."

Rupert's voice echoed up and down the deep brick stairwell. Rosalind leaned against the wall, folded her arms in front of her, and glowered at him.

"I completely forgot about that," said Rupert. "I guess you can't let him in?"

"I don't have a key, Rupert," replied Luke. "At least, not yet."

"Oh yes, of course," said Rupert and scratched his head. "Okay. Can you ask him if he'll hold on for me? Or come back? My dear friend Rosalind is about to show me a dead body."

Rosalind rolled her eyes and sighed loudly.

"Hang on. I'll check with him," said Luke. Rupert heard snatches of conversation in the background.

"He says he can come back in an hour if you like," said Luke finally. "What do you want to eat tonight?"

"That's great," replied Rupert. He looked at the time on his phone. It gave him over two hours to get back home. "Are you cooking again? Or we could go out. Do you like sushi?"

"Love it," said Luke. "There's a new place in St. George's Wharf. We could sit by the river and watch the sun go down."

"You old romantic, you." Rupert laughed. He looked across at the thunderous expression on Rosalind's face and hurriedly turned away from her. "I'll see you in a while," he whispered. "Can't wait to see you again."

"Me too," replied Luke. "You going to fuck me before dinner or after?"

"Both," whispered Rupert. "I'll make sure we're better prepared this time."

He ended the call and looked across at Rosalind.

"So," she said. "It seems the love life has picked up."

"That's the guy who lives upstairs," replied Rupert. "His bath overflowed and brought my ceiling down. So I've had to—"

"Spare me, please," said Rosalind. She unfolded her arms and reached for the handrail of the next staircase. "Let's get you down to the morgue before you make me any later."

"Ah," said Rupert.

In truth, he had plenty of time before he needed to return to see the man from the insurance company. But Rosalind had already given him the autopsy report. The unveiling of a dead body under his nose was not something he relished. And the one time she had shown him the morgue, she had been very theatrical, relishing his discomfort.

"I'm so sorry, Rosalind," he said. "Luke was ringing to say the insurance man is waiting for me back home. If I don't leave now, I'll miss him."

"Well really, Rupert," said Rosalind. "I put myself out for you time and time again. And what do I ever get—"

She was interrupted by Rupert's phone ringing again. Rupert looked at the screen. It was police officer Will Sutherland.

"I'm sorry Rosalind, I'm going to have to—"

"Oh, fuck off, Rupert," said Rosalind, and she stomped back up the stairs.

Rupert answered the call and hurried down the stairs. He desperately needed some fresh air.

"Hi, Will, what have you found?"

"Not a lot," replied Will. "He's got a student visa, valid for another year. His address checks out as the apartment upstairs to your place, and he's got an international driver's license. No criminal convictions. He'd be deported immediately if he did something dodgy anyway."

"Does it say where he's from in America?" asked Rupert.

"I can't pursue the inquiry much further than this, Rupert," said Will. There was a hint of irritation in his voice. "I'd have to put in requests to the Home Office and the US authorities. It would be too risky for me."

"How come the police released him if he'd lost his memory?" asked Rupert. "Surely he'd be handed over to a hospital for a psych check?"

"It seems a woman came into the police station to vouch for him. She was his psychiatrist. It all checked out, so they released him."

"What's her name?"

Will hesitated. "I'm not sure I can give that to you. It's a major breach of confidentiality. If you were to follow through and talk to her—"

"Is she based at London Psychiatry Partners?"

Again Will hesitated. Rupert tried a different approach. "You don't have to say yes or no. I'll ask the question again. If you hang up the call, then she's based there. If you stay on the line, then she's not."

Rupert reached the bottom of the stairs. He pushed open the heavy fire doors and breathed in the fresh air.

"Was the person who vouched for Luke from London Psychiatry Partners?"

The line went dead.

IT WAS another scorching-hot afternoon, and Rupert decided to take advantage of the good weather. There was a rental cycle rack a few minutes' walk from the hospital, and it would be a pleasant twenty-five-minute ride along the River Thames back to the apartment. He set off for the cycle rack at a brisk pace and brought up the cycle app on his phone to confirm there were cycles available.

He had just arrived at the cycle rack when his phone rang.

"Where the fuck are you? The afternoon editorial's about to start, and iron knickers is gunnin' for yer."

"I'm at Fulham mortuary, examining a dead body," Rupert replied. It was almost true. "Why does she want me there? I'm on the suicide assignment for Special Reports. Remember? She took me off news."

"'Course I fuckin' remember," replied Sandra loudly. "I was there when she did it. But she says you're followin' up some story about mass killin's from the NCA. So she wants you to brief everyone on it. Is that right?"

"Yes," he said. "And you can tell the charmless Eileen that pathologists don't plan their diaries around the BBC's afternoon editorial meetings—"

"Don't take it out on me, darlin'," said Sandra. "I'll tell her you're fuckin' the arse off your gorgeous American and can't be bothered to come in." The line went dead.

Rupert was furious. He shoved the phone in his pocket, unlocked one of the red cycles, and jerked it from the stand. He had not planned to share Jerry's information with the rest of the hacks in the newsroom. Angrily, he mounted the bike and set off along the street. It was his scoop. How dare the news editor tell everyone about it before he had time to complete his research and write the synopsis for the story? Now his colleagues would be reaching for their phones and calling their contacts around the country. Thanks to Eileen, some of them would steal a lead on the story from him.

A lone taxi driver honked his horn furiously and overtook Rupert at breakneck speed. Lost in his thoughts, Rupert had let his cycle drift across the otherwise empty street. He veered to the side of the road and stopped. His heart pounded. The taxi screeched to a halt, reversed until it pulled alongside, and the driver directed a torrent of abuse at Rupert through his open window.

As Rupert breathed deeply, the taxi roared off. Rupert tried to shift the anger he felt for his newsroom colleagues onto the belligerent taxi driver. But the face of Eileen Jones kept reappearing in his mind. He resented her attempt to share his investigation with the rest of the journalists. He suspected he was heading for another showdown with Eileen. And he knew in his heart he would lose, because of her seniority. Whatever the prestige of the BBC and the attractions of living in London, having a bully for a boss was no picnic. Maybe he should simply cut his losses and go for the CNN job. A couple of years out of London might not be so bad.

RUPERT PULLED up at the entrance to the cycle docking station beneath Vauxhall Arches. He dismounted and walked the length of the gloomy Victorian archway in search of a free space in the rack. A lone busker with a guitar sang a mournful rendition of Ralph McTell's classic "Streets of London." The singer was probably no more than twenty. His long tangled hair hung down beneath a battered black porkpie hat. Rupert fumbled in his pocket for some loose change and threw a few pound coins into the open guitar case in front of the young man. Rupert had been a busker himself in Barcelona the summer after he finished university. It had been more a show of rebellion against his parents than a desire to rehearse his musical ability. His talent, he knew, was limited, certainly by the standards of the young man busking under the Vauxhall Arches today.

He parked the cycle in a space near the end of the docking station and walked away from the arches. As he walked along South Lambeth Road, he texted Luke: *Five minutes away*

He hesitated before he added two kisses and sent the text. Was he the only one who regularly pondered the subtext of the messages he sent? A moment later, his phone vibrated with a response: *Great. I couldn't say on the phone, but the guy's hot! XOXO*

Rupert was puzzling over what was behind Luke's reply when a follow-up message arrived: *But very straight.* Followed by a sad-faced emoji. Rupert's laugh brought a look of panic to the face of an elderly woman walking toward him, and she gave him a wide berth as they passed each other.

The five lanes of traffic on South Lambeth Road were stopped at the lights, and he quickly wove his way across the lines of stationery vehicles to the other side of the street. Paton Road was fifty yards down to the right. Rupert looked down at his phone and began to compose a reply to Luke.

"Mr. Pendley-Evans."

Rupert looked up and stopped abruptly. His path was blocked by the same man who had accosted him outside Broadcasting House earlier.

"Are you stalking me?" asked Rupert.

"Not at all," replied the man. "But I need to speak to you urgently. Can we talk now?"

"If it's about Luke, I'm going back there right now," said Rupert. "Why don't you come and say whatever it is you have to say to both of us?"

The man took a step back and shook his head with exaggerated emphasis.

"Oh no, no, no. Not a good idea." He reached into his pocket and pulled out a business card.

"Tomorrow," he said. "I can meet you anywhere. Anytime. Call me on this number. It's imperative you don't tell Luke."

He pushed the small white card into Rupert's hand and walked on quickly. Rupert spun around.

"Wait," he called after the retreating figure. "What the hell is all this about?"

The man broke into a run and nimbly wove between the lines of slow-moving traffic on South Lambeth Road. Rupert stopped at the side of the street. If he gave chase now, it would make him even later for the meeting with the insurance assessor. He looked down at the business card he had been left with. On it was written the name Christian Mark Matthews, followed by a mobile telephone number. There was no address. No company name. Rupert shoved the card into his pocket, turned, and headed for Paton Road. Despite what the man had said, Rupert was determined to discuss it with Luke when he got back home.

LUKE WAS right. The insurance assessor was certainly hot. He was sitting on a solitary wooden chair in the entrance hall of number 54 when Rupert pushed open the front door. In his late twenties and well over six feet tall, he wore black motorcycle leathers. His jacket was open and revealed a white T-shirt beneath. He stepped forward and extended his hand in greeting.

"Mr. Pendley-Evans?" said the assessor. "My name's Jack Alexander, from Bradshaws."

Jack had a firm handshake. There were beads of sweat on his forehead, and they ran down the sides of his face. The front of his white T-shirt was wet and clung to his skin. It highlighted the definition of his well-developed pectoral muscles. Jack released Rupert's hand and wiped his brow with the sleeve of his leather jacket.

"Apologies for being like this," he said. "It's bloody hot on a motorbike in this weather. But you've got to wear the leathers, haven't you? Especially in London. I'm on the bike 'cause my wife's due imminently with our second child. I'm on standby to get back home if the baby starts to come."

"No problem," replied Rupert. "I'm a biker myself. Is that your Triumph parked outside?"

"Yeah, that's right," said Jack. He picked up his helmet and small rucksack from the hall floor. "And is that your BMW? Very nice. I really should get rid of my bike. Now I'm a father."

"Oh, don't do that," said Rupert. He took his keys out of his pocket, opened the front door of his apartment, and turned to look at Jack. "We could go for a ride out sometime."

"Really?" asked Jack. He followed Rupert into the apartment. "This probably sounds really naff, but you're the guy on the news, aren't you? The one who did the story last year about the end of the Royal Family?"

Rupert sighed. He was never going to shrug off the notoriety the story had created for him. And why had he just made a pass at Jack? It was clearly true what Luke said. The man was very straight. He had a wife and nearly two children. But for Rupert, when confronted with a sexy man like Jack, it was almost instinctive. Perhaps he better stick to the matter at hand.

"It's the bedroom ceiling," he said. "Follow me."

He led the way down the corridor to his bedroom and pushed open the door. A musty, damp smell hit his nostrils immediately.

"Oh wow," said Jack. He stood in the doorway and looked around the room. "It's a hell of a mess, isn't it?"

He set his rucksack on the floor, opened it, and pulled out a tablet computer and a camera.

"This won't take long," he continued. "I'll just check through the form you completed over the phone the other day and take a few photos. Then I'll be off."

He began to take photographs of the water damage. Rupert backed out of his way, unable to take his eyes off Jack's figure-hugging leathers as he crouched down to get a good angle.

"Hey, guys. I thought I heard voices."

Rupert looked up to see Luke's face peering through the gaping hole in the ceiling. Jack turned and waved an acknowledgment.

"Hi, Mr. Diamond," he said. "Thanks for your help earlier." He looked across at Rupert. "You didn't tell me this guy was a TV star."

Jack winked at Rupert, who was taken aback when a glow of embarrassment warmed his cheeks. The emotion caught him by surprise. He could usually maintain a mask of serene composure.

"I'll see you in a few minutes, Rupert," said Luke. "Hey. While you're there, do you think you could get those things from your bedroom we needed the other night? You don't want to make a second journey."

Luke gave a broad grin and tapped the side of his nose. "I'll be ready whenever you are." His face disappeared from the hole in the ceiling.

Rupert looked across to see Jack wink at him again. That glow of embarrassment turned from warm to red hot. Rupert awkwardly attempted a smile and hurriedly left the bedroom.

CHAPTER 16

WHEN RUPERT entered Luke's apartment twenty minutes later, he could hear a track playing by the same American artist from the night before. He checked that his mobile was switched to silent and put it down on the hall table.

"Let's be happy together, your dreams become mine, as my dreams become yours…."

Rupert slipped off his jacket and hung it on one of the coat hooks fixed to the wall by the front door. He walked down the hallway to the living room and pushed open the door.

"Luke?"

There was no sign of the American. Rupert dumped his rucksack on the floor. He bent down and pulled a small wash bag from it. He stood up and walked back down the corridor to his bedroom.

"Together in everything we hear and see. Together from now until eternity…."

"Luke?"

Rupert paused at the entrance to his bedroom and turned to the door opposite. The door to Luke's bedroom. It was open a few inches, and Rupert could see the room was in semidarkness. The rhythmic *whap-whap* of the rotary fan was the only sound from within. He eased the door open wider. The curtains were almost completely closed. A narrow slit between them allowed a shaft of late-afternoon sun to fall across the bed. On it lay the naked form of Luke. He was on his front, his face turned toward the door. When the hinges creaked, his eyes opened, and he looked up at Rupert.

"Hey, sexy Englishman," he said in a sleepy voice. "Sorry. I didn't mean to doze off like that." He rolled over on his back, put one arm behind his head, and gave Rupert a lopsided smile. "I wanted to be ready for you when you returned."

Rupert looked down the length of Luke's body to his erect penis.

"Looks like you are ready for me," said Rupert. "I don't think I've done sex in the afternoon for a long time."

Luke slid across the bed away from Rupert and patted the space beside him. Rupert stepped from the doorway. He dropped the wash bag beside Luke and stood next to the bed.

"The essential supplies you asked for."

Luke unzipped the bag and pulled out a small bottle of lube and a handful of condoms.

"Large," he said, appreciatively. "Well, I guessed that was the case last night."

He sat up and cleared the bag and its contents onto the cabinet next to the bed. Then he turned over, slid back across the mattress toward Rupert, and pulled himself into a kneeling position. His face was a few inches away from Rupert's. He leaned forward, and they kissed. Gently at first, their soft lips colluded in subtle connection. Luke twisted his head, parted his lips, and extended his tongue in a slow exploration of Rupert's mouth.

Rupert reached for the buttons of his shirt and began to unfasten them one by one. Luke's warm hands slid under his shirt and reached for the buckle of his belt. Rupert abandoned his shirt buttons and put his arms around Luke's shoulders. He pulled the American's head closer to his, opened his mouth wider, and thrust his tongue deep into Luke's mouth.

Luke clasped his hands on either side of Rupert's head, pushed it back firmly, and held it a few inches away from him. He stared intently at Rupert's eyes, his breath brushing Rupert's face with rapid gusts of moist, warm air.

"I want you to fuck me," he whispered. "On the edge of the bed. And I want to be able to look deep into your eyes as you do."

He pulled Rupert's head close, and Rupert lovingly scanned every contour, every imperfection, every line of beauty of Luke's face. He used his thumbs to trace the hollows beneath Luke's prominent cheekbones, while Luke ran his fingertips slowly around the edge of Rupert's sharply defined beard down to the flat edge of his chin.

Luke lowered his head and used his tongue to map the taut muscles of Rupert's neck. Several times he opened his mouth and pulled on the flesh, tender love bites that drew gratifying sounds of pleasure from Luke. An erotic wave spiraled from Rupert's neck, down through his chest, and into his groin. His cock swelled tight against his briefs, as though impatient to be released. Luke expertly undid the remaining buttons of Rupert's shirt and slipped it from his shoulders. He continued to slide his tongue down Rupert's torso until he arrived at his right nipple, where he lingered to engulf it in a damp, fervent embrace.

Rupert moaned in appreciation. He rapidly tugged his arms out of the sleeves of his shirt and flung it to the floor. He placed his hands on Luke's inner thighs, close to his groin, and massaged the soft flesh with his fingertips. His fingernails abraded the skin, and the action brought a satisfying groan of gratitude from Luke. He slid his tongue across Rupert's broad chest and stimulated his left nipple as he held it delicately with his teeth.

"Fuck." Rupert exhaled the word in a slow, ecstatic release. "My nipples are directly connected to my cock. You're fucking good at that."

Luke repositioned himself to sit on the edge of the bed, with his feet flat on the floor. He rapidly unbuttoned Rupert's fly and pulled both his trousers and briefs down to his knees in one swift move. With his arms supporting him on the bed, he sat back to admire Rupert's hardened cock, gently pulsing in front of him.

"Damn, it's large," he said with admiration. "I'm gonna have to get lubed up to feel that deep inside me."

Luke lay back on the bed and reached an arm behind his head to find the small canister of lubricant. He edged forward, raised his legs high in the air, and used the gel to prepare himself. Rupert kicked off his shoes and struggled to get his trousers and briefs the rest of the way off. He hopped from one leg to the other as the tight-fitting cloth grudgingly released him.

Luke peered between his legs at the spectacle and laughed. "Socks, Rupert. I'm certain I've never been fucked by a man wearing nothing but his socks before, and for sure I'm not going to start now."

Rupert looked down and shrugged. "I hoped you might have lived in England long enough to understand our sexual deviancies." He bent down and pulled off his socks. "Okay, then. Just for you."

He lifted his bare foot to rest on the edge of the bed between Luke's legs. From there, he pointed his toes downward until the ball of his foot met Luke's cock. He arched his tendons to apply pressure, and Luke stiffened and flexed beneath him. Luke released a sigh that embraced contentment and anticipation in a single exhaled breath.

Rupert took hold of Luke's legs, which were still raised high in the air, and rested them on his shoulders. Luke raised his torso and leaned forward, his abdominal muscles pulling taut as he reached for Rupert with a condom in his hand. He slid the sheath carefully over the head of Rupert's engorged penis. A look of concentration crossed the American's face as he slid the edges of the condom down the full length of Rupert's cock. Luke applied lube to the condom and spread it over the tip. He wrapped his fingers around the shaft of Rupert's penis and spread the lube liberally along its length. Rupert leaned back as the persistent stimulation generated an ecstatic wave deep inside his body.

Luke guided Rupert's cock gently, yet firmly, into place. The two men gazed at each other for several seconds before Luke finally spoke.

"This feels so right, Rupert," he said. "It must be the greatest expression of trust and affection two men can show for each other. I need you deep inside me. Now."

Rupert breathed deeply. He was used to urgent, animal lovemaking. This was altogether more sensuous. More measured. More... loving. He slowly thrust his pelvis forward and entered Luke.

THE BEDROOM was in semidarkness, lit by the glow of a single street lamp shining through the gap between the curtains. Rupert blinked several times and peered into the gloom. Luke lay beside him with his back to Rupert. He had pulled his knees into his chest and wrapped his arms tight around a pillow. Rupert ran his fingers gently along the smooth, firm skin of Luke's exposed forearm. The American's breathing quickened, and he released a contented sigh. Rupert slipped his arm under Luke's, pulled his body in close, and allowed his torso to follow the curve of Luke's back. The warmth of his skin and the even rhythm of his breathing were comforting and calming. Rupert kissed the nape of Luke's neck and tasted the residual saltiness of dried sweat on his skin.

He kissed Luke's neck again. He stirred, and stretched his body against Rupert's, compressing his cock and causing it to stiffen once more.

"Hey, sexy Englishman," said Luke. He yawned. "Are you wanting more? I'm not sure I can manage right now."

Rupert kissed Luke's neck a third time and held him tight.

"I'm good like this," replied Rupert. "For someone who says he can't remember anything, you've got one hell of a muscle memory somewhere inside that sexy body of yours. I've not had sex as good as that. Ever, I think."

Luke raised his arms and turned his body gently until he faced Rupert. Their foreheads rested against each other's, and Rupert could see Luke's deep brown eyes glint in the sodium-yellow light of the street lamp.

"Do you think I'm better than the cute insurance man from this afternoon?" asked Luke.

"What on earth made you think of him?" Rupert pulled his head back to stare at Luke in puzzlement. "I hardly gave him a second look. Especially when he talked so much about his wife and family. He's straight."

Luke stretched his head forward and kissed Rupert on the lips. He rested his forehead against Rupert's again and sighed. "Oh, but if you could turn him? Wouldn't you be tempted?"

Rupert shook his head. "People are the sexuality they are, Luke. It's not a choice. They can't be 'turned.'"

Luke pouted and wrinkled his nose. "You're right, I guess. I'm just being dumb." He reached forward and kissed Rupert again. "I'm so glad I flooded your bedroom. Otherwise I wouldn't have had three of the happiest nights of my life."

"You're a beautiful, passionate, and tender lover." Rupert punctuated each adjective with a kiss to Luke's lips. "That's surely not the first time for you? Have you really no memory?"

Luke groaned, nestled in closer to Rupert, and ran his hand gently down the side of Rupert's face. "I don't know. Perhaps I've been a very bad boy, and I've blanked a guilty past from my memory."

"That reminds me," said Rupert. "I've been warned off you. Twice today."

Luke pulled his head back to stare at Rupert. "What do you mean?"

Rupert rose to lean on one elbow. "There was this guy. Once outside the BBC and then again this afternoon when I was coming back here. He told me I'd damage you if I continued to see you."

Luke sat up. He turned and reached to switch on the bedside light. Rupert shut his eyes against the sudden glare.

"Why didn't you say anything earlier?" asked Luke. "Who was he? Did you ask him why?"

Rupert sat up as well and slowly reopened his eyes. He shielded them with his hands and peered through the splay of his fingers at Luke. The American was staring at him, his eyes wild with alarm.

"Hey, hey," said Rupert. He reached out and put an arm around Luke's shoulder, placed his free hand on the side of Luke's head, pulled it toward him, and stroked it gently. "It's okay. I don't know who he is. He gave me his card, and I was planning to call him to fix a meeting tomorrow. I want to talk to him. Maybe he can give us some clue about your memory loss."

Luke lifted his head away and stared at Rupert with a look of fear in his eyes. "What if we find out something terrible? Maybe I've done something really bad in the past. If that's true, I don't think I want to know. Do you?"

CHAPTER 17

RUPERT STARED forlornly at the handwritten message on the noticeboard in the entrance to Vauxhall Tube station.

> We are sorry, but all northbound Victoria Line trains are suspended due to a person under a train at Oxford Circus.

Rupert needed to be in Islington by nine o'clock. He was meeting the head of research at the charity Manwatch. The journey by Tube would have taken at most twenty minutes. His only alternative was a taxi. At this time of day, it would be a slow journey. At least forty minutes, if not more. He was going to be late. Again. He swore out loud, and several passengers around him nodded in mutual melancholy.

At the taxi rank in South Lambeth Place, there was already a line of more than a dozen people waiting. They checked their mobile phones impatiently. Rupert joined the line and called Manwatch. He reached the inevitable voicemail and left a message.

It was half past eight in the morning, the peak of London's rush hour. The traffic noise around him was deafening. Added to that was the insistent thump of a pile driver. Work had begun on the foundations for yet another luxury apartment block. Even at this early hour, the air was warm and sultry. Above him, the sun shone from a cloudless sky. It was going to be another scorching-hot day. Rupert had never known a summer of heat as intense as this in Britain. London smelled like a continental city instead of its usual damp, musty staleness. People walked by wearing bizarre combinations of summer outfits. Rupert could never understand why so many British men wore long socks with open-toed sandals. In his opinion, it was tantamount to a crime.

Luke's concern for what he might find out about his past preyed on Rupert's mind. What if the American had done something seriously bad? What if he was a criminal? The mind had clever ways of blocking out the memory of catastrophic experiences. It could shut them away in deep recesses of the brain. Perhaps Luke's psychiatrist would unlock them. But what of the consequences for Luke if she revealed to him he had committed some heinous deed? Luke was already—well, not neurotic, but certainly excitable. And his strange reaction to video screens was something Rupert had never encountered in a person before. Such a revelation could tip Luke over the edge.

At times like this, Rupert wished he still smoked. The whole process of lighting a cigarette, placing it in his mouth, and tasting and smelling that first, glorious puff was a distant happy memory. He had quit shortly after leaving university, shocked by the slow, painful death of his grandfather from lung cancer.

A few people in the taxi line puffed on e-cigarettes. Rupert thought they looked comical. They sucked on their plastic tubes, then exhaled a swirl of white mist around them, resembling children, trying to appear grown up. But perhaps Rupert envied what he missed.

A long conga line of black cabs finally turned the corner into South Lambeth Place, and the line of people waiting in front of Rupert rapidly diminished. Within five minutes, he was at the head of the line for the next taxi to arrive. He thought again about Luke's fears for his past. Something else puzzled Rupert. How could an art student have over a quarter of a million pounds sitting in his bank account? Was it there legitimately? Perhaps Luke was the beneficiary of some major bank raid. Or maybe a drugs deal.

At last, a taxi pulled up alongside Rupert. He opened the door, gave the driver the address for Manwatch, and climbed in. As he pulled the door shut behind him, the driver accelerated rapidly into the London traffic, and Rupert tumbled back into the seat. He picked up his rucksack from the floor where it had fallen and checked his wallet was still safe inside. Which was when he found the business card for Christian Mark Matthews. With a forty-minute journey ahead of him, now was the time to give the mystery man a call.

"I DON'T think we're goin' anywhere, mate," said the cab driver, staring at the line of stationary traffic ahead of him. "Do you want to 'op out 'ere? It's about five minutes' walk, I reckon."

Rupert glanced at the clock above the cab driver's head. It was a quarter to ten. The journey across London had taken nearly an hour, despite the taxi driver seemingly trying every shortcut through London's narrow backstreets he could find. They were currently opposite Angel Tube station at the start of Islington's chic and fashionable Upper Street. Rupert looked out the window at the rows of cafés, street-food sellers, designer-clothing boutiques, and organic-food outlets. Strange to think it was known as "The Devil's Mile" in Victorian times, on account of the high levels of crime and prostitution in the area. Rupert loved London's quirky history, and he found it hard to think of living anywhere else.

He paid the driver and headed off on foot for the offices of Manwatch. They were on the top two floors of a large Georgian building near the top end of Upper Street. Despite his regular gym regime, Rupert was panting by the time he reached the reception desk.

"You all right?" asked the receptionist. He was a young man wearing a telephone headset and a figure-hugging T-shirt emblazoned with the single word Versatile in bright red letters.

"I'll be fine after a glass of water," Rupert said. "I've come to see Jonathan Swain. And I'm horribly late."

"I think Jonny's just gone into another meeting." The receptionist peered at Rupert closely. "Oh, you're the guy off *Special Reports* who reckons the Royal Family's dead in the water. Bet they love you, mate."

Rupert said nothing, but he regarded the young man with the look he reserved for traffic wardens and tax inspectors.

"I'll see if he's free," said the receptionist hastily. "There's a water cooler in the corner. Take a seat."

Rupert gulped down two plastic cups of water and sat on a shabby-chic leather sofa, in which most of the springs seemed to be broken. To pass the time, he picked up the glossy brochure for Manwatch and read its introduction page.

> Manwatch was founded in 2001 to tackle the twenty-first century's crisis in masculinity. Our aim is to highlight and campaign for greater recognition of the problems men face: in the home, in the workplace, and in education. Through research, we demonstrate the crisis facing modern men in Britain, as masculinity is redefined, and man's role in society is undermined through unemployment, questions of sexuality, and men's traditional role in the home.

"Rupert Pendley-Evans?"

Jonathan Swain was a tall, gangling man in his early thirties. He wore a check shirt, brown corduroy trousers belted tightly at the waist, and tan loafers with no socks. His mop of brown hair was curly and unkempt, and his face wore an expression of intense concentration, made more severe by a pair of large gold-rimmed spectacles. Rupert stood and extended his hand in greeting.

"That's me," he said. "Jonathan Swain? I'm so sorry for being late. The Victoria Line was suspended, and the traffic's been awful—"

Jonathan Swain dismissed the apology with a wave of his hand. "No matter, Mr. Pendley-Evans." He grasped Rupert's hand and shook it with exaggerated enthusiasm. "I'm at your disposal. We're very excited to have the opportunity to tell this shocking story of male suicides to your television audience. How can I help?"

"Well, there'll be the practical issues to sort out," said Rupert. "We want to film an interview with someone from Manwatch. And take some general shots around your offices. But the main thing we need is a couple of case studies. It's the people's stories that will communicate the impact of this to our viewers."

Jonathan Swain pushed his glasses up the bridge of his nose and peered at Rupert earnestly. "Yes, yes, I can see that. But it's the figures you need to understand first. My job is to collate the data, and I can tell you, they're shocking. A record number of young men are dying." His eyes lit up with excitement as he reeled off a list of statistics. "Suicide is the number one killer of men aged 18–30 in Britain today. Not drugs, not car crashes. But suicide. The reasons are many. Firstly, advertising. It's no longer women who are made to feel inadequate about their image. About their bodies. Advertisers now target young men. There's been a rise of over 25 percent in beauty products aimed at men. Add to that the problems of growing unemployment in the adult male population. As high as 30 percent in some parts of the country—"

"Yes, but—"

"Then there's the changing definition of masculinity." Jonathan Swain was in full flight. "Did you know that 44 percent of young LGBT people have considered suicide? Boys do worse than girls at school, leading to lower educational ability among men in adulthood. That leads to lower achievement in the workplace. And this government hasn't got a clue. They're even talking of reintroducing National Service."

"Sure, sure. I get that," said Rupert. He was rapidly cooling toward Jonathan Swain. The man was obsessed with data and statistics. Rupert needed human interest. If he returned to the newsroom without at least one juicy case study, Eileen Jones would make his life an even greater hell. "Can you help me with filming some stories to illustrate this? I need interviews with relatives or friends of suicide victims? That sort of thing."

"Yes, yes, all in good time," said Jonathan. "Come down to my office. I've got our strategy presentation to show you. It's very exciting."

Rupert's heart sank. It was going to be a long day.

THE TEXT message was brief and arrived thirty minutes into Rupert's meeting with Jonathan Swain.

Missing you. When are you back today? Going to Dr. Ballantyne this afternoon. I'll fix supper tonight. XOXO

The message prompted Rupert to take charge of the meeting. He pushed the Manwatch head of research to get to the point. Rupert was annoyed with himself for allowing Swain to sidestep his requests for specific details on stories he could film for the documentary. He must be getting soft all of a sudden, he thought to himself.

"Jonathan," he interrupted. "Your presentation is fascinating. But I can read all this myself. I don't have time now. If you want the BBC to feature your research on *Special Reports*, the best thing you can do is come up with two case studies. We need to tell the stories of families of suicide victims, or ideally the story of someone who found themselves on the brink. If you can't help me with that, I'm going to have to go to Samaritans instead. I know they've done similar research, and we've used them before."

Jonathan Swain was clearly stung. But the threat worked. Over the next hour, Rupert gathered together a list of contacts and recommendations from two of Jonathan's colleagues. He sat with a Manwatch researcher as she telephoned two families and persuaded them to allow the BBC to film their story. Meanwhile, another researcher gave him the names of three men who had attempted suicide and said she was confident they would give him interviews.

By the time he left the building at midday, Rupert was a lot happier about the shape his documentary was taking. But he needed to make up for lost time and set up the filming with the contacts before they changed their minds. He took out his phone and made a call to Christian Mark Matthews. He was going to have to postpone their meeting.

"Hello, Rupert. Where are you? I'm here in the café in Little Portland Street."

"Yes, I'm sorry. I've had a really difficult morning, and I'm running very late. Can we postpone until tomorrow? I've got a few things I need to sort out on this story."

There was silence at the other end of the phone. Rupert began to walk toward Angel Tube station.

"I don't think you understand the severity of the situation," Christian said at last. "I need you to understand the danger Luke is in. You're not taking this seriously."

Rupert stopped walking. "How can I take it seriously, when you've not told me anything so far? What danger is he in?"

"I'm not going to tell you over the phone. It's probably not safe. I need to see you in person."

"Look," said Rupert with mounting exasperation. "You accost me in the street two days ago and warn me off seeing Luke. You tell me he's in danger, but you won't tell me why. Just who the hell are you?"

After another long pause, Christian replied, "Mr. Pendley-Evans, Luke is my brother."

CHAPTER 18

THE CAFÉ was crowded and noisy. Adie's All Day Breakfast Bar was halfway down Little Portland Street, a narrow, sunless thoroughfare overshadowed by a clutter of midrise office buildings on either side. Even on this bright sunny day, very little light penetrated the windows of Adie's. To add to the gloom, the café was poorly lit by four fluorescent strips suspended from the high ceiling.

Adie's meals were cheap, simple, and plentiful. Its owner, Adrian Such, was Australian. Loud, cheerful, and very tall, he shouted instructions over the heads of the café patrons to his long-suffering staff. Rupert loved the food, loved the prices, and loved the atmosphere Adrian created. It was a good venue for confidential discussions. A stone's throw from the BBC's news headquarters in Langham Place, the café was bustling and noisy. Rupert's clandestine meetings were unlikely to be overheard.

He stood in the doorway and scanned the occupants of the fifteen or so wooden tables crammed into the small space. Christian Mark Matthews sat on a barstool at the far end of a narrow counter set against the window. He cradled an empty coffee cup in his hands and stared into the street. Rupert walked over and laid a hand on his shoulder.

"Hello again," he said. "Can I get you another one of those?"

Christian started and almost fell off his stool. He stood and turned to shake hands with Rupert in the narrow confines of the café. Close-up, Rupert thought Christian looked older than he remembered him in his brief encounters in the street. Heavy lines furrowed his forehead, and dark shadows underlined his eyes. As he extended his hand in greeting, Rupert noticed how his shoulders sagged. He was beginning to stoop like an old man.

"Mr. Pendley-Evans. It's great you came. I know you guys in television are real busy all the time."

Rupert was not an expert on American accents, but the man sounded like he came from a Southern state, maybe South Carolina or Georgia.

Christian turned briefly to glance at his coffee cup. "I'll skip another coffee. I've had three already. But can I go get you one?"

Rupert shook his head. "Let's just get straight to it." He pulled out a second stool from under the countertop and sat. "Why didn't you say you were Luke's brother in the first place?"

Christian fumbled with his own barstool and climbed back on it clumsily. "There's much I can't tell you, Mr. Pendley-Evans—"

"Call me Rupert. Please."

"Sure. Rupert. And none of this must get back to Luke. He doesn't know I'm here in London."

"Why not?" asked Rupert. "If you're here to protect him, as you say you are, surely he needs to know he can call on you?"

Christian sighed. He looked at Rupert and said nothing. Rupert held his gaze steadily. As a TV reporter and interviewer, he knew the importance of silence. It encouraged interviewees to open up and reveal more than perhaps they had intended. Neither man spoke for what seemed like nearly a minute. It was Christian who broke the silence first.

"Luke has had a very severe mental trauma," he began. "I brought him to London to receive the best psychiatric care I could find. And also to remove him from his...." Christian paused as if searching for the right words. "To remove him from his environment."

"What happened to him?" asked Rupert. "And what was his 'environment' as you call it?"

Christian shook his head. "I can't tell you, I'm afraid. The less you know about his previous life, the better. That's if you insist on continuing to see him."

"Of course I do. He's a very special person. I've only known him for a few days, but I can honestly say I've never met anyone quite like him."

"You are...." Again, Christian paused to find the right words. "You are attracted to him, are you?"

"Yes."

"Physically?"

Rupert frowned. "Is that a problem for you?"

Christian coughed. He fumbled in his jacket pocket and pulled out a packet of throat lozenges, then unwrapped one and popped it in his mouth. "Even in the height of an English summer, I get a cold. Look, Mr. Pendley-Evans—"

"Rupert."

"I'm sorry." Christian coughed again and corrected himself. "Rupert. I'm not sure Luke is quite ready for anything like that right now. You see—"

"I don't agree," Rupert interrupted. "What he needs is love. I think I can give him that." Rupert was surprised at how easily the words tumbled from his mouth. "What he needs is to know more about his past. And you've told me almost nothing. So, Mr. Matthews, will you answer my questions? Or should I go back home right now and tell Luke I'm being warned off him by his brother?"

Christian looked panicked and laid a hand on Rupert's arm. "Don't do that. It could kill him. I mean it."

Rupert looked down at his arm. He glared back at Christian, who hastily removed his hand and rubbed his face nervously.

"Okay, Rupert," he said. "The truth is, back home Luke was in danger. Real danger. It's what caused his mental breakdown. I brought him here. Set him up in the apartment. With the shrink in Harley Street. But even this far away, there's still a risk they'll come after him."

"Who's they?"

"The people who want him dead."

Rupert was taken aback by the words. He felt a cold sensation run down his back, and his mouth went dry. He had not expected to hear this. If indeed it was true.

"You have to tell me more, Christian," he said. "Who exactly are they? And why do they want him dead?"

One of the waiters tried to push past them, carrying a tray piled with plates of food. When he saw Rupert, his eyes lit up and he stopped.

"Hey, Rupert," he said. "How's it going? Still pursuing the Royals, are you?"

Rupert attempted a smile in response to the young man's untimely interruption. "Hey, Michael. Good to see you. Oh, you know. Bigger fish to fry now." He tipped his head toward the tray of food. "Don't let me hold you up."

Michael grinned and continued on past. Rupert turned to Christian, raised an eyebrow, and waited for a reply to his questions.

"I've been advised by his psychiatric team," said Christian, "that Luke is best helped if he rediscovers his own memories, with only gentle prompts. If too much is revealed too quickly, it could bring about a major breakdown. If I tell you about his previous life, there's a chance you'll tell Luke." Christian stared at Rupert. His eyes looked sad, without hope. "He's my brother. I let him down once. I can't risk doing it again."

Rupert shook his head. He looked away and stared out the window. A road sweeper negotiating his way up the narrow street caught his attention for a moment. The man guided his machine past pedestrians jostling for their own little parcel of personal space.

"You're telling me nothing," said Rupert finally. "If you care about him so much, why are you avoiding him? And why does Luke react so violently to video screens? That scared the hell out of me the first time it happened."

"I'm part of the reason for his present condition," said Christian. "Me and the rest of his family. Did he find the photograph?"

Rupert stared back at Christian. "So it was you who put that photo in his portfolio case? Why?"

"I've offered photographs of his former life to his therapist. I hoped they might trigger memories for him. Memories of happier times. But she refused to show them to him. She said it would be too risky. She was worried that, if he reacted badly, she'd lose his trust. So I thought it might help if he simply discovered one. Did he say anything about it?"

"Not much," replied Rupert. "He just said he'd found it in his case. So, that's Luke with his family? You. His parents. And do you have two sisters?"

Christian nodded. "That was taken fifteen years ago. Before it all started."

"Before what started?"

Christian sighed and stood up. "I can't. I don't know you well enough to trust you. Maybe in time—"

"How much time?" Rupert stood as well, his face a few inches from Christian's. Now he could see the family resemblance. Before him stood a vague imitation of Luke. An older, sadder version of Luke.

"If he's in danger," Rupert continued, "aren't I entitled to know more? What if something happened to him? And you could have helped save him by telling me more? Now? How would that prey on your conscience?"

Christian hesitated. Rupert thought his words, and maybe the passion in his voice, had caused Luke's brother to rethink. But Christian simply said, "You have my number. And I have yours. Let's stay in touch."

RUPERT LEANED back in his seat, stretched out his legs, and rested them on his desk. It had been an exhausting and sometimes frustrating afternoon. But his documentary was, at last, taking shape. He had spent over four hours on the phone and persuaded several potential interviewees to take part in the filming. The stories he had listened to were harrowing. The young men he had spoken to told tales of rejection, dejection, and desperation.

One of the stories had stuck in Rupert's mind. It was told to him by a thirty-two-year-old man from a small town in the north of England. He was gay. This was presumably the reason why his story had resonated so much with Rupert. The man had been brought up in a family who went to a Pentecostal church. The man loved going to the church because it was warm, welcoming, and because he liked the music. It was also an escape from his father. Until he was thirteen years old, his father had beaten him regularly. His mother deferred to her husband and told her son to "be a man." The beatings stopped when he was thirteen because he had grown big enough and strong enough to fight back. His father no longer hit him but continued to belittle him, to call him useless and deny him any love.

The man sought solace in the church and confided in one of the elders that he was gay. That was when he was forced to make a choice. The elder told him he would have to leave the church if he continued to say he was gay. The man chose the church because it was familiar, and because he craved its support and acceptance. He continued to deny who he was for five years, until his internal struggle became too much to bear.

It was one of the church elders who found him. On the steps of the church. An empty bottle of his mother's antidepressants still in his hand. During his recovery in hospital, he confided his conflict to a male nurse. The nurse recommended an LGBT counseling service in the nearby city of Leeds. It was the start of a five-year journey of personal understanding and acceptance.

Rupert was close to tears by the end of the telephone conversation. At least the story had a happy ending. The man had moved to London, far away from his family and far away from the church. Through his love of music, he had joined the London Gay Men's Chorus.

"You know," the man said. "When I first arrived there and felt the love and acceptance that the chorus gave me, that's when I discovered what real love means. I could just be me, without being judged. That's the love my family and the elders of the church should have shown me."

Rupert thought about the conversation. It would make a strong, emotional case study in his documentary. He compared the man's family experience to his own. Rupert's father had never beaten him. His parents had been difficult when he came out, but they dealt with it by not talking about it. A very British approach. Rupert resented the unspoken rejection but had come to terms with it. He daydreamed about the time when he might take Luke to meet Mother and Father. He had never introduced any of his boyfriends to his parents before. Maybe this time.

Rupert picked up his phone and called Luke. There was no answer. He let it continue to ring, but the voicemail failed to cut in. He redialed, and once more it rang without an answer. Rupert looked at the time. It was nearly 6:30 p.m. Luke said he was cooking supper that evening. It was time for Rupert to get back and see what was happening in the kitchen.

"HI, HONEY, I'm home," called Rupert in what he thought was his best imitation of an American accent. He slammed the door shut behind him and strode down the hallway to the kitchen. A pan of water was simmering on the stove, and there were sliced onions, garlic, and peppers on a chopping board next to it. But no sign of Luke.

He went into the living room, where the electric fan moved the warm late-afternoon air around in an illusion of cooling.

"Luke?"

Rupert walked back down the hallway to Luke's bedroom. He passed the open bathroom door on his way. He glanced into the spare room opposite, before entering Luke's bedroom. The room was empty, but the loft hatch was open and the slim metal ladder pulled down. Rupert walked over to the ladder and rapidly climbed the steps to the studio. He stood on the top rung and looked around the brightly lit space. There was no sign of Luke. Still perched on the top of the ladder, Rupert took out his mobile and called Luke's number. Once more, the phone rang without being answered. No voicemail cut in.

Luke had disappeared.

CHAPTER 19

RUPERT'S HEART was pounding. He sat at the top of the ladder and took deep breaths. All he could think about was the sentence Christian had spoken that afternoon in the café: *"The people who want him dead."*

Had those people finally caught up with Luke?

Of course, there were plenty of plausible explanations for Luke leaving a pan of water boiling on the stove, and they did not involve villains seeking his demise. Luke could have gone to the shop on the corner to get some vital ingredient for the supper he was cooking. He might have gone for a walk and forgotten to turn the heat off under the pan before leaving.

Or he could have been abducted.

Rupert had not seen any sign of a struggle in the apartment. Nothing was smashed. Everything seemed to be in its place. But "they," whoever they were, could easily have grabbed Luke as soon as he opened the front door. They would have no need to enter the apartment. Rupert decided he had to assume the worst. If Luke's brother was not being melodramatic, and Rupert had no reason to believe he was, then he needed to act quickly. Before anything happened to Luke. Rupert called Christian and listened with frustration as the phone rang without answer. After six rings, the voicemail cut in. Rupert hung up and tried again. Again it switched to voicemail. He left a message and ended the call.

For several minutes he stared at the phone. The depth of his anguish surprised him. He had only known Luke for, how long was it? Five days. And yet. The excitement he had felt at the prospect of seeing Luke this evening when he entered the apartment. The sense of contentment he had felt first thing this morning with Luke lying in his arms. The panic and feeling of loss he felt now. He knew what it all added up to, and it terrified him. Until he met Luke, Rupert had had other ambitions for his life, and they had not included falling in love.

Still at the top of the ladder, he decided on his plan of action. He would go out and look for Luke. He would start with the corner shop. It was only five minutes away. After that, he would come back here and somehow track down Luke's brother. But why was Luke not answering his phone? He must have it with him, or Rupert would have heard it ring in the apartment. Unless it was switched to silent. Perhaps it was broken, or the battery had died. There were plenty of innocent explanations. But right now, Rupert could only fear the worst.

He turned around on the top step of the ladder and carefully climbed back down to the bedroom. He was uncertain how he would find Christian, but he was confident he would succeed. He might have to put himself into greater debt with police officer Will Sutherland. Before then, he would simply keep trying to call Luke's brother. Rupert went back into the kitchen to turn off the heat under the saucepan of water. He was about to head for the front door, when his phone rang.

"'Ello, sweetheart. You all right?"

Rupert leaned back against the worktop and sighed. "Hello, Sandra. Yes, I'm fine. What can I do for you?"

"Well, it's more a case of what I can do for you," Sandra replied. "You won't 'ave seen this yet, 'cause it's come through one of the BBC local radio stations. There's been another one of them killin's."

Rupert's shoulders sagged. His heart began to pound once more, and he took a deep breath before he asked his next question.

"Where?"

"Out in Kent," Sandra replied. "Down in Chatham, on the Thames estuary. A bloke found 'angin' again. Like the one in Chiswick."

Rupert's heart rate quickened further. "Do they know who he is?"

"They ain't officially identified 'im yet. But the reporter says 'e worked at the radio station. 'Elpin' out and stuff. It's a bit of a gruesome scoop for 'em. 'E was really young. Only twenty."

Rupert let out an audible sigh of relief and opened his eyes. He felt sad for the young man, but at least it could not be Luke.

"That's great, Sandra," he said. He straightened up and headed for the front door of the apartment. "Thanks for the advance warning. I'll talk to my contact at the National Crime Agency. Then I'll talk to Eileen. She's surely got to see this is a much bigger story than the Manwatch report. That makes five deaths now."

He reached the front door, opened it, and stepped out onto the landing. He checked his pocket for his keys before he slammed the door behind him and strode down the stairs two at a time to the hallway. Luke might be missing, but at least he was not another reported victim. Not yet.

"By the way," added Sandra, "I was talkin' to Betty in the Washington bureau just now. She told me to say she's sorry she ain't got back to you about that photograph. There's been another resignation at the White House, and they're all goin' apeshit in the bureau at the moment. But she says she knows where the picture was taken."

Rupert paused on the front step of the house, poised to close the door behind him.

"Where was it taken?"

"It's some university down in Virginia. They were only filming there the other week, so she remembers it distinctly. It's called Liberated University. She says that picture must 'ave been taken a few years ago, 'cause they've built a new bit on the side since then. But she's definite that's where it is."

Rupert slammed the door shut behind him and began to jog down the street in pursuit of Luke. Liberated, VA had been stamped on the crucifix Rosalind Goodman found on the body of the student who hanged himself in Chiswick. Somehow, Luke was connected with that same university. Rupert's hunt for the missing American had just gained a fresh urgency.

CHAPTER 20

THE TAPE measure snapped shut. The young man pulled the pencil from behind his ear and noted the measurement on his clipboard. He climbed down the small set of metal steps he had brought with him, moved them a few feet to the left, and climbed back up again. He reached up to the ceiling and took another set of measurements.

The man was in his midtwenties. His pale blue overall had the words Helping Hands embroidered on the back in large white letters. On the front, in smaller letters, was his name, Horacio Serrano. The overall fit snuggly. It pulled tight against his crotch as he stretched up to hold the tape measure against the broken ceiling of the bedroom. Each time he extended his arms above his head, the overall's zip unfastened a little bit more, revealing that Horacio wore no T-shirt underneath. Luke watched, fascinated, as the curly black hair on Horacio's chest poked through the ever-widening opening of his overall as the zip crept down toward his crotch.

"Hola?" queried Horacio's voice from above him. "You see something you like?"

Luke glanced up to see Horacio smiling at him, his deep brown eyes crinkling at the corners. He tipped his head. To add emphasis to his point, Horacio reached down with one hand and briefly cupped it around his cock. He grinned and, with the same hand, pulled on the zip of his overall to close the front and hide from Luke the temptation of his chest. Luke glanced away in embarrassment, but he was unable to resist taking one last, furtive glance at the Spaniard's crotch.

Horacio jumped down from the small set of metal steps. He stood directly in front of Luke and took a note of the latest set of measurements. He looked up and winked. "It's a big hole to fill, señor," he said, "but you can be sure it will be a good job. I can start for you right away if you want." His perfect teeth flashed white in another broad grin, and he pulled down on the zip of his overall to reveal a hint of chest hair.

"No, no," replied Luke, and he stepped back toward the open door of Rupert's bedroom. "My friend's gotta get three estimates for the insurance company. Just email him your price, and he'll pass it on."

Horacio stepped forward and again stood directly in front of Luke.

"And you don't want me to start right now?" he asked, his smile lighting up his face. "I work very fast. Or we can wait until your friend, he get back. Then we can—"

"No, no," said Luke, and he stepped to the side of the doorway. He did not know why, but Horacio's obvious advances had unnerved rather than flattered him. "I've got to get back upstairs. I just remembered. I left something boiling on the stove."

Luke showed Horacio to the front door. He made sure the young Spaniard had Rupert's email address. Once more he resisted the man's enthusiasm to stay and closed the door on him. He hurried back up the stairs to his apartment and went inside. In the kitchen, he was relieved to find the pan of water he had set boiling to blanch the spinach had not boiled dry. But he was surprised to discover he had turned off the heat before he left the apartment. He was certain it was on when he left to show the builder into Rupert's apartment.

He looked at the wall clock. It was half past seven. He had expected Rupert to be back by now. Luke would have called Rupert if his mobile phone had been working. But dropping it into the sink while he was washing the vegetables was possibly the dumbest thing he had done that day. The phone was now on the sill of the living room window, hopefully drying in the dying rays of the afternoon sun. To accelerate the drying process, Luke had also turned the electric fan on and aimed the stream of air at the phone. Tomorrow, he might find out if it still functioned. He had dunked his phone in water once before, but that time he had rescued it before any real damage had been done.

Luke went into the living room to check on the phone. Superficially it looked fine, but he decided not to risk turning it on again until tomorrow. He crossed to the CD player and put on a recording of Ella Fitzgerald. The sound of "My Funny Valentine" filled the room. He sat on the couch, stretched out his legs, and put his hands behind his head as he allowed the golden voice to envelop him in its warmth. Luke closed his eyes tight shut and imagined Rupert's arms wrapped around his body, the tip of his tongue nuzzling the nape of Luke's neck. The past five days had been both ecstasy and agony for Luke.

Since February, he had just about held it together. Many times he had awoken in the middle of the night, alone and terrified of the aching loneliness inside him. He had made a few friends in the last months. But none of them were close friends, people he could confide in. If he still had close friends, the memory of them was gone. The only person who knew his deepest fears was Jemima, his psychiatrist. He had spent hours describing to her the nightmares he experienced. The terrifying daydreams that exploded in his head whenever he caught sight of a video screen. She listened carefully, politely, almost reverently. She gave him coping strategies. Small routines to help him deal with his demons.

That all changed when he met Rupert.

Rupert filled his heart. That was the only way he could describe it. Even now, as Luke lay stretched out on the couch, he physically ached for Rupert to return. Despite his amnesia, Luke could not believe there was a former time in his life when he had felt so completely contented. A time when he had been so rich in emotion, with no other desire than to live in the immediate present. With Rupert as a part of his life, he was confident he could finally confront his fears. Together, they could resolve the mystery of Luke's forgotten life. In his mind's eye, Luke pictured a time when he and Rupert would board a plane together, return to America, and he would be reunited with the life behind the heavy curtain of his shrouded memory.

Luke sat up and opened his eyes wide. It was the first time he had consciously considered returning to America. Until now, America had been just another country on the map. For a brief moment, it had seemed like his homeland. And that felt good.

The front door opened and, a moment later, slammed shut. Luke heard footfalls in the hallway. He stood and turned to the living room doorway.

"Hey, Rupert," he said. "How was your day? I'm fixing dinner, really I am. I just came in here to get some music on."

Rupert's face looked thunderous. He stood in the open doorway, his mobile phone in his hand. His chest rose and fell rapidly, and he breathed heavily.

"Where the fuck have you been?"

CHAPTER 21

THE WHIRRING of the electric fan behind Luke sustained a steady bass line. Its slow, easy rhythm contrasted with Rupert's uneven, angry panting as he gasped for breath. Against this soundscape, the noise of Luke's blood pumping throbbed in his head. His ears seemed about to burst from the pressure. His chest was tight, and his own breathing was shallow and panicked.

Luke could think of nothing to say. Rupert's arrival and immediate outburst had shocked him into silence. A moment ago he had been planning a journey to America with a beautiful man. A man he had only met five days ago but who had already changed his outlook on life. A man who had given him hope, comfort, and a passion for life, love, and long, sustained sex. That should have been the same man who stood before him now.

But the man in front of him was an alien. Anger had exploded from Rupert's lips. Those lips that only a few hours ago had hungrily explored every inch of Luke's body. Rupert's eyes held a look of fury. Those eyes, which over the past five days had melted Luke's very being each time he gazed into them.

Luke inhaled deeply and held his breath for several seconds. He allowed the inhaled air to escape slowly, resisting his body's urge to gulp a fresh intake. It was a technique Dr. Ballantyne had instructed him to use. The throbbing in his ears diminished a little. He repeated the procedure—once, twice, three times. Finally, he was confident the moment of panic had receded, and he could resist his base instinct to simply run from this new threat. He gripped the arm of the couch to steady himself. He swayed slightly and felt his legs weaken. The reassurance of the couch's solidity bolstered his confidence.

"I was showing the final builder your bedroom," he said. "You remember? I offered to stick around today so I could let them in. Even though I had to reschedule my appointment with Dr. Ballantyne." Luke turned to face Rupert square on. He straightened his legs, arched his back, and stood tall.

"And I fixed supper," he continued. "So. What the fuck's gotten into you, Rupert?"

"I didn't know where you were," replied Rupert. "And you didn't answer your phone."

Luke walked across to the windowsill and picked up his mobile for Rupert to see. "I dropped it in the sink this afternoon. I'm drying it out." He put the phone down, turned to face Rupert, and folded his arms in front of him. It was instinctive. But he knew it was a clear signal of his mood. "So I should check in with you every hour? Always be by the phone, waiting for your call? Is this how relationships work with you, Rupert? You've gotta somehow own me? 'Cause if it is, you can fuck off right now."

"No. I didn't mean—don't get so defensive," said Rupert. "I was worried about you. I've got good reason—"

"I'm a big boy, Rupert. I've managed perfectly fucking well for the last six months before you showed up. And frankly, I've got enough to think about without having to cope with your mood swings—"

"Mood swings?" Rupert stepped into the living room and stood by the end of the couch. He too folded his arms in front of him. The two men squared off to each other. The last rays of the evening sun reflecting off them heightened the drama of the moment in Luke's mind.

"Yeah, mood swings," replied Luke. "Do you know what I was thinking, before you stormed in like a fucking hurricane? I was thinking we could go away together. I could take you to America. To my home." He could see the words made an impact on Rupert. "Yeah, that's what I said. My home. Surprised to hear me say it? I sure was. But then you storm in and stand there like you think you fucking own me or something—"

"That's not what I meant," countered Rupert. "I don't think I own you. I know I don't own you. And if you want to talk about mood swings, then take a look at yourself, why don't you? My phone rings and you run away like a...." Rupert's voice rose in both pitch and volume. "Like a frightened deer, for God's sake. One minute you say, 'Oh, I'm complicated,' and then the next you're suddenly all over me like a rash."

"That's fucking mean." Luke was shouting now. Had he been deceived by Rupert's previous affection? He no longer had confidence it was sincere. "I've spent six months learning to trust people. It takes time. Do you know how much I've been hurt?"

He paused for effect, but not for an answer.

"No, you fucking don't. I really thought... in the last few days... since I've met you... it's been like...." Each phrase escaped Luke's mouth like air from a deflating balloon. His shoulders sagged, he dropped his arms to his side, and he opened the palms of his hands in supplication. "What's your fucking problem, Rupert?"

The ringing of Rupert's mobile punctuated the moment. Its effect on Luke was immediate and violent. His chest pulled tight until his ribs stopped him from breathing. His vision clouded, and the walls of the room felt as if they were closing in on him. He had to escape. Saw the open doorway and knew he had to run before his legs gave way and he would no longer be able to run.

"No you don't." Rupert leapt forward and wrapped his arms around Luke. He threw him to the ground and pinned him down with the weight of his body. Luke struggled to escape. He could hear the ringing of Rupert's phone, which had landed close to them, and he could feel its vibration through the floor near his head. He twisted his head away from the noise. He had to avoid looking at the screen. If he did, the voice would start. The voice that told him to do terrible things.

"It's a phone," said Rupert. His hot breath was on Luke's face as he spoke. His head was just inches away. "Nothing more, Luke. There's nothing to be afraid of. Why are you afraid? Open your eyes. Look at me."

Rupert was shouting now.

Luke screwed his eyes tight shut. He dare not look at the screen. Rupert could not make him. He could not be that cruel. Luke struggled to escape from Rupert's hold. He arched his back and pushed hard against Rupert's hands.

The touch of Rupert's lips against his own made him freeze. It was as if an electric charge shot through his body. The tightness in his chest eased, and he opened his mouth to inhale a gasp of air warmed by Rupert's breath. Luke exhaled, and at the same time allowed his muscles to relax. The phone continued to ring and vibrate close to his head. But it no longer held any power over him. He inhaled, and Rupert's tongue gently caressed the perimeter of his lips. Finally he opened his eyes and gazed into the deep blue of Rupert's, staring down at him from inches away.

"You're safe," breathed Rupert, the edges of his face crinkling in a smile. "I won't let them harm you."

Luke lifted his head and kissed Rupert on the lips.

"Thank you." He mouthed the words silently.

Luke lowered his head back onto the floor and turned to stare at the mobile phone. It shook violently from side to side as it vibrated and rang. After two more rings, it finally stopped. Luke looked at Rupert and repeated the words again. "Thank you."

With Rupert on top of him, Luke's groin stirred. He pulled his arms free from Rupert's restraint and wrapped them around the Englishman's shoulders instead. The two men opened their mouths, and the anger of a moment ago morphed into passionate kisses of forgiveness. Rupert slipped his hands under Luke's shoulders and cradled his head above the floor. He squeezed his shoulders tight so that together they shared the very air they breathed. The bristles of Rupert's beard dug into the surface of Luke's skin, over and over again, as they rolled until Luke lay on top of Rupert. He tugged his arms from beneath Rupert's shoulders and extended his hands along the length of Rupert's arms until he had them pinned to the floor. Luke gazed down at the panting figure beneath him. Rupert's cock pushed hard against his own, and he swiveled his waist in a slow gyration, enjoying the sensation that coursed through his body. Enjoying the pleasure he was giving Rupert.

Once more, the ringing of the mobile phone punctuated the moment. Both men froze as the shrill sound stabbed the air. Luke slowly relaxed his grip on Rupert's arms. He pulled himself into a kneeling position astride Rupert and reached for the phone, which lay facedown on the floor. He picked it up, flicked it over in his hand, and looked at the screen. Turning to Rupert, he said, "It's someone called Christian."

Rupert took the phone from Luke and looked at him with a puzzled expression on his face as he answered the call.

"Hi. ... No, I'm not. ... Yes, that was him. He's right here. Do you want to...? ... Sure. ... Sure."

There was a long pause as Rupert listened intently. Luke reached forward, placed a hand on Rupert's chest, and massaged gently. Rupert used his free hand to take Luke's and intertwine their fingers.

"We can go to my parents," said Rupert finally, still speaking into the phone. "They're out in the country—Buckinghamshire. Northwest of London. I can text you the address. ... So what do you think might...?"

Rupert tried to sit up. Luke rolled off his chest and lay back on the floor beside Rupert.

"We have to tell the police," Rupert continued. "No. Listen. If that's what you think, then you have to tell the police. ... Why not?"

Rupert scrambled to his feet. He walked over to the far corner of the living room and held the phone close to his mouth. Luke sat up and strained to hear what he was saying. "Christian, you have to tell me more. Who is the...?"

Rupert paused to listen to the response. He looked across at Luke.

"Don't you think you have a responsibility to him? You know he's right here. Why don't you tell him yourself? ... I don't care. If you won't, then I will."

Rupert ended the call and shoved the phone in his pocket. He leaned against the wall and folders his arms in front of him. There was a look of fury on his face.

"Who was that?"

Rupert ignored the question. He reached back into his pocket, pulled out his mobile, and sent a text. Luke got to his feet and crossed the living room to stand in front of Rupert. He placed his hands on Rupert's waist and gently tugged him forward.

"Rupert. Speak to me," said Luke. "What's happened?"

Rupert rested his forehead on Luke's and wrapped an arm around his waist. He gazed into Luke's eyes and sighed. "You really don't know who Christian is?"

"No. Who is he? It sounds like you've told him we're going to your parents. We've only known each other five days. Don't you think that's a little...?"

Rupert leaned back and laughed. "Yeah. Definitely. And it will be a first. Fuck knows what Father will say."

"But why?" asked Luke. "What's happened?"

Rupert placed his hands on Luke's as they rested on his waist. He leaned forward from the wall and took one of Luke's hands in his.

"Come on," he said. "I need to show you something."

He led Luke down the corridor to the bedroom, sat Luke on the bed, and crossed to Archibald on the wooden dresser. From Archibald's lap, he picked up the photo and carried it over to Luke.

"Look closely," he said. "What do you see?"

Luke stared at the photograph and examined each face in turn. He looked up at Rupert and shook his head.

"Look at the boy on the far right," said Rupert. "Look at him closely."

Again, Luke stared intently at the photograph. The shape of the boy's face. The way he stood. He looked vaguely familiar.

"Luke," said Rupert gently. "It's you."

The photograph blurred in front of Luke's eyes. He blinked several times and tried to refocus on the image. His heart rate quickened, and the sound of his own blood pounded in his ears again. His eyes flicked rapidly from one face to another, but they were ultimately drawn to the severe lines of the face in the middle of the photograph. Unfocused though it was, he knew. His shoulders shook, his fingers loosened, and the photograph fell from his hands. He looked up at Rupert's face, partly obscured by the tears that flooded his eyes. Rupert reached forward and pulled Luke's head to his chest. He enveloped him in his arms and allowed Luke to sob.

Wave after wave of long-stifled emotion flooded out of Luke. He held tight to Rupert and simply allowed himself to vent his anguish. Minutes passed. Rupert tenderly stroked Luke's head, as a mother or father might console their distraught son.

Finally, Luke's shoulders stopped shaking, and his breathing became more controlled. He wiped the tears from his eyes and looked up at Rupert.

"You've got to help me," he said. His body gave another involuntary shudder of emotion. "I hate him so much."

CHAPTER 22

THE LEATHERS Rupert brought for Luke were a snug fit. They clung tight to almost every part of his body. Luke admired himself in the full-length mirror. He turned side on. They felt good. He had to admit it. They looked damn good. Tight, black leather jeans enhanced the bulk of his thighs and the narrowness of his waist. They sagged a bit in the ass, but Rupert explained that was necessary to allow Luke to sit comfortably on the motorbike. Luke turned up the collar of the black leather jacket and closed the zips on both sleeves. Kevlar protective panels in the back, sleeves, and shoulders of the jacket filled out the upper part of his torso, adding bulk to his hours of work in the gym. He crossed to the bed and sat to pull on the reinforced bike boots, fasten their zips and Velcro covers.

Luke smoothed his hands across the surface of the leather stretched tight across his thighs and grinned at a stirring in his groin. The sensation both surprised and pleased him. He stood, and the rigid shape of the boots forced him to lean forward, like a skier about to descend a black run. He attempted to stand straight, the upper part of his body compensating for the enforced bend in his knees. The jeans pulled tight against his crotch, and his cock rose to the stimulation of the leather hugging his body.

"Sexy man." Rupert's voice came from the doorway. Luke turned. Rupert wore a one-piece racing suit made of red leather. White leather panels stitched into it enhanced the shape of his torso and legs. He crossed the bedroom to stand behind Luke at the mirror and placed his hands on Luke's thighs. "I've not worn those leathers for a long time." He studied Luke's reflection in the mirror with an admiring grin. "They fit you really well. How do they feel?"

Luke took Rupert's hands in his and pulled them to wrap around his waist. "They're making me horny," replied Luke. "I was getting a hard-on just standing here, even before you came in."

Rupert slipped his hand down and caressed the front of Luke's leathers. "And now you're rapidly outgrowing those jeans. By the second, it feels like."

He placed both hands on Luke's shoulders and pulled him gently forward. He bent his head and kissed the side of Luke's neck, slowly and tenderly, his tongue warm and moist against Luke's skin. "I could fuck you right now, the way you look and feel," breathed Rupert. "But we've got to get moving. It should take us only an hour and a half to get there. But my parents go to bed early. I don't want to upset them by arriving late." He raised his head from Luke's neck, to look at him in the mirror. "Especially when I'm bringing you as well."

"Are they going to be okay about it?" asked Luke.

Rupert shrugged. "Who cares? They'll have to put up with us. What's important is your safety." He gave Luke one final kiss and squeezed tight on his thickly padded shoulders. "Have you packed what you need?"

Luke turned to the bed, picked up a small rucksack, and showed it to Rupert.

"That's good," said Rupert. "The BMW's got decent-sized panniers, but there's a limit to how much you can get in. The crash helmets are downstairs. Let's get off."

"Have you got room for this as well?" Luke picked up his half-size folio case. "If you haven't, I'll hold it for the journey. But if we're staying there a long time I need to draw."

THEY CRESTED the brow of a small hill, and the sign for Middle Claydon flashed in the headlight of the motorbike. Night had fallen. As the bike sped along the tree-lined lanes of Buckinghamshire, Luke breathed the clear, cold air, which was laden with the scent of damp vegetation. He had never ridden pillion on the back of a motorbike before, and he found the experience exhilarating.

The sun had not quite set when they left London, and the city's streets were still crammed with cars. Late commuters made their way home after long working days. Rupert expertly wove the powerful BMW motorbike in and out of the streams of traffic. He filtered to the front of lines of cars so they could get away quickly when the lights changed to green. At first, Luke clung tight to Rupert's waist. He followed Rupert's instruction to lean when the bike leaned and not to fight against it. Luke felt good holding Rupert close, and he followed each move of the Englishman's body. It was as if they were one with the bike. Before long, Luke relaxed his grip on Rupert's waist and settled back to enjoy the sheer power and independence the motorbike afforded them both.

When they reached the open roads outside central London, Rupert opened the throttle wide. The powerful bike roared and carried them west. Ahead of them, the final glow of the sun painted the sky a vivid and rapidly darkening orange. Mile after mile melted past, and they soon left the urban sprawl of the dormitory suburbs behind. They sped on to the Chiltern Hills and rural north Buckinghamshire, once home to the poet John Milton and the author Roald Dahl.

In Middle Claydon, Rupert rode the bike slowly past the King's Arms in the heart of the village. In the pub garden, they could see crowds of drinkers enjoying the balmy summer evening. After a hundred yards, Rupert turned off the road and steered the motorbike through a wide stone gateway onto a gently arcing driveway. The road led under a canopy of mature beech trees, until they cleared to reveal a wide, Gothic-style mansion, its facade badly cracked. The ivy covering it threatened to completely obscure some of the upper windows.

Rupert brought the motorbike to a halt and cut the engine. He held the machine steady as Luke stood up on the side pegs and dismounted. Luke fumbled with the strap securing his helmet until Rupert turned to him and expertly unfastened it. With the helmet off, Luke stared at the scale of the mansion in front of him.

"I thought you said your parents were farmers." He tried to count the windows that ranged along the front of the house. He figured it was over twenty. "You didn't warn me how rich they are. I didn't pack a tuxedo or anything."

Rupert laughed. "You're not going to need one. But the helmet will come in useful when Father throws one of his tantrums."

Rupert climbed off the bike, placed his helmet carefully on the ground, and unhooked the panniers.

"Come on," he said. "It's time to meet Lord and Lady Pendley-Evans."

"RUPERT, DARLING," said Lady Pendley-Evans. She kissed her son lightly on either cheek. "Why didn't you tell us you were coming? I haven't had time to make up the bed in the spare room."

She turned to Luke.

"And you're Rupert's little friend, are you?"

"Good evening, Lady Pendley-Evans," said Luke. He was uncertain whether to bow or not, so he dropped his head forward slightly as he shook her hand.

"How charming," said Lady Pendley-Evans. She turned back to Rupert as she continued. "We so rarely meet any of our son's friends. You'd almost believe he was ashamed of us."

The door to their right rattled open, and a red-faced man with a tangle of wispy white hair on his head emerged into the dark, wood-paneled hallway.

"Good God, what are you doing here?" Lord Pendley-Evans asked Rupert. "You haven't been gone a week. Do you need money again or something?"

"Father," said Rupert, "this is my friend Luke. We've come to stay for the weekend."

Lord Pendley-Evans snorted and looked Luke up and down. Rupert's father had a disconcerting way of turning his head away from whatever he was looking at so he appeared to observe everything from the far corner of his eyes.

"Another biker, I see," he said. "Presume you'll be terrifying the pheasants tomorrow. Bloody bad time of year to unsettle them. Just before the shoot starts."

Rupert ignored his father and turned to Lady Pendley-Evans. "Don't bother about the spare room, Mother. Luke will sleep in my room with me."

"But darling," said Lady Pendley-Evans, "there's only one bed in your room."

Rupert said nothing. His mother avoided her son's gaze and turned to her husband. Lord Pendley-Evans had opened the glass front of the grandfather clock and was adjusting the hands.

"Clarence, darling," she said. "Have you removed all your rubbish from the old cottage now? I think the boys will be much more comfortable down there. Away from the house." She turned back to Rupert. "Have you eaten? There isn't a great deal I'm afraid. Cook had one of her purges of the larder this afternoon. I could probably make you a sandwich if you're hungry."

"Don't bother," he said. "We'll go down to the old cottage and sort it out. And maybe raid the kitchen in a while. Why don't you and Father head off to bed? There's no need to worry about us."

"Darling, it's not yet ten o'clock," protested his mother. She turned her head slightly and raised a finely drawn eyebrow at him. "We're not completely gaga, my dear." She patted him on the shoulder. "Now, make sure you and—" She turned to Luke with a quizzical look.

"Luke, ma'am," he said obediently.

"Yes of course it is. You make sure you and young Luke don't get up to any mischief down in the old cottage. We don't want complaints from the villagers, do we?"

"SHE IS something else," said Rupert. He threw open the door of the old cottage and felt inside for the light switch. "You'll have to ignore my bloody parents." He walked inside the cottage, dropped his bag on the floor, and hung his crash helmet on a coat hook next to the door. "Did you see the look she gave me? When I said you were sleeping with me? What century does she live in? So she forces us to come out here rather than be under her roof."

Luke followed Rupert into the dimly lit cottage. He hung his helmet alongside Rupert's and looked around. The front door opened directly into a small living room, filled with oversized furniture, which made it feel even smaller. On the opposite wall, another door opened onto a small kitchen. There was a narrow staircase to the left of the front door. The cottage smelled musty, with a hint of wet dog and stale cabbage.

"Hey, Rupert, this is great," said Luke. "Your mom did the right thing. We're away from the house, so we don't have to be well-behaved." He dropped his rucksack to the floor and pulled Rupert toward him. "Hey, Mr. Grumpy." Luke used his thumb and forefinger to push up the edges of Rupert's mouth. "Are you going to give me a smile with those beautiful lips? For me?"

Rupert took Luke's forefinger into his mouth, sucked on it slowly, and winked.

"That's better," said Luke. He tugged the zipper of Rupert's race suit down to below his waist, reached his hand inside the suit, and felt for Rupert's cock. "Hey, Mr. Leatherman. You're wearing a jock? That's making me horny."

He removed his hand from Rupert's mouth and kissed him hungrily on the lips. Rupert undid the zip of Luke's jacket and slipped his hands inside the waistband of his jeans.

"Maybe you're right," Rupert whispered into Luke's ear. "Let's misbehave right now. Come on upstairs. Have you ever fucked in leather? There's nothing like it."

He broke away from Luke, picked up his bag from the floor, and headed for the staircase. He paused with one foot on the first step and held up the bag. "Come and fuck me. I've got everything we need right here."

Rupert ran up the stairs, followed closely by Luke. At the top, the staircase opened directly into the only bedroom in the cottage. Rupert threw himself back onto the bed, and Luke fell on top of him. Again, he reached his hand inside the front of Rupert's leather race suit and found Rupert's cock, warm and firm. Rupert massaged the front of Luke's leather jeans, and Luke's cock strained to be released. Luke rolled off Rupert, shifted to the side of the bed, and stood up. He fumbled to unbutton the fly of his jeans. Rupert rose into a kneeling position on the bed, shoved Luke's hands out of the way, and expertly undid the buttons. He pulled down Luke's jeans and briefs and leaned forward to lick the tip of Luke's cock. Turning his head sideways, he opened his mouth wide and took Luke's penis deep inside. Luke groaned and placed his hands on Rupert's head appreciatively. Rupert manipulated with his tongue and throat for several minutes, until Luke was ready to explode in orgasm. Just as he was about to come, Rupert pulled back. He had a condom in his hands, which he expertly slid over Luke's rigid cock and down the shaft.

"Not yet, my American beauty," said Rupert. "I want you to save that until you're inside me."

Rupert climbed off the bed, pulled the leather race suit off his shoulders, and allowed it to fall until it hung below his waist. Luke's orgasm slowly receded, but his cock remained stiff. The sight of Rupert stripped to the waist, his bike leathers hanging around his solid thighs, was a powerful aphrodisiac. His cock twitched with anticipation, and its tip felt hypersensitive even beneath the numbing sheath of the condom. Rupert pulled a bottle of lube from his bag, finished peeling off his clothes, and prepared himself to receive Luke. He massaged his own cock and looked down at Luke's.

"Go gentle with that," he said. "It's beautiful, but it'll take a moment for me to accommodate you." Rupert leaned his forehead against Luke's and gazed into his eyes. At the same time, he gently caressed lube along the length of Luke's cock.

"You're the best thing that's ever happened to me," breathed Rupert. He kissed Luke once on the lips, turned, and positioned himself over the edge of the bed. Luke gingerly pushed forward to enter Rupert. He encountered resistance at first and paused. After a moment, Rupert relaxed around him, and Luke tentatively entered more deeply. His penis was given a warm embrace as Rupert took him deep inside. Luke leaned forward and grasped Rupert around his shoulders.

"You okay?" he whispered into Rupert's ear. The Englishman groaned in assent.

Luke began to swing his hips gently back and forth, and he worked his cock inside Rupert. An overwhelming sensation of pleasure and oneness overcame him as he penetrated deeply. Rupert gripped and released him and matched the rhythm of Luke's thrusts. Luke came to the brink of orgasm far quicker than he expected.

"Fuck, Rupert," panted Luke. "I can't hold back much longer."

"I'm ready," said Rupert. His breathing came in short, explosive bursts. He massaged his own cock, and Luke could tell he was ready to unite with him in orgasm.

A spasm of ecstasy took over Luke's body, and his pelvis thrust without control. Beneath him, Rupert shuddered as he ejaculated. Rupert's grip on Luke's cock tightened, which sent his body into another spasm of sheer pleasure. Their bodies fused in passion for over a minute, until the waves of violent muscle contractions reduced to ripples. Luke collapsed onto Rupert's back, and he kissed Rupert's neck. With his cock still inside Rupert, he knew blissful unity.

Rupert turned his head sideways and reached his hands back to rest them on Luke's thighs. "Don't tell me you've not done that before."

Luke laughed and kissed him again.

A woman's voice called from below.

"Rupert, darling. Are you upstairs?"

Rupert tensed and squeezed Luke's cock again.

"For fuck's sake," whispered Rupert. "What's she doing here?"

The voice of Lady Pendley-Evans sounded closer. "I felt so guilty after you left, darling, I've brought some leftover game pie for you and your little friend. Shall I come up?"

CHAPTER 23

LUKE BALANCED the plate of game pie on Rupert's chest and reached across for his glass of wine on the bedside cabinet. Rupert lay back on a pile of pillows. His eyes were closed, and he massaged Luke's thigh with his hand.

"Your mother makes an awesome game pie," said Luke. He took a sip of wine and pulled a chunk of pheasant meat from the remains of the pie. "I don't think I've ever tasted anything like it."

"She didn't make it," mumbled Rupert. His eyes were still closed. "Mother can't boil an egg. Jeanette cooks everything."

Luke finished chewing on the meat and swallowed. "Is she your cook?"

"Much more than that," said Rupert. "Jeanette's been around ever since I was born. She and her husband, Frank. They're lovely. Jeanette helps Mother, and Frank works on the farm with Father. Before I was sent to boarding school, I used to spend hours with Jeanette in the kitchen. Or I'd walk the farm with Frank. Anything to avoid being with Father. All he ever did was shout at me and tell me I was useless."

He opened his eyes, lifted the plate from his chest, and put it on the bedside cabinet. After rolling onto his side, he laid his hand on Luke's chest and wove his fingers through the curls of black hair.

"And now we need to talk about you," he said. "Maybe we can make good use of the time we've got here. Away from London. Come on, Luke." His fingers stopped. "Maybe after what happened this afternoon, you'll start to remember more."

Luke turned to Rupert. The Englishman watched him intently. He looked so hopeful, so optimistic. Luke felt guilty about letting him down.

"I'll try real hard," he said. "But I've spent months with Dr. Ballantyne, trying to remember. And so far I've turned up a big fat zero."

"Until today," said Rupert. "Think back to the photograph this afternoon. It's been sitting in Archibald's lap for days. And yet, when I pointed out it was a picture of you with your family—"

Luke's chest tightened as he recalled the image of the man in the middle of the smiling group of people. His breathing quickened, and he grasped Rupert's hand to his chest.

"Why do you hate your father so much?"

Luke shook his head. He couldn't connect the picture with the idea of family. All he knew was that the face instilled a cold, terrifying sense of fear inside him.

Rupert gently squeezed Luke's hand. At the same time, he reached for his mobile phone on the table beside the bed and held it between them. Luke was dazzled by the glare from the screen. It shone directly in his eyes. His heartbeat quickened further, and beads of sweat formed on his forehead. But he kept control. This time he forced himself to stare at the screen. After a few more seconds, Rupert dropped the phone onto the bed. He reached forward and cupped his hand affectionately around Luke's face. Luke took hold of Rupert's hand and kissed its palm over and over.

"Oh, sweet man," said Rupert tenderly. "We're finally making progress. Slow progress. But having seen the terror that phone caused you only yesterday, you were incredibly brave just then."

Luke blinked, and tears formed in his eyes. "Are you saying I've wasted my time at Dr. Ballantyne's?"

Rupert shrugged. "Let's just say you couldn't have done that a day ago. What was it that frightened you so much about the phone before? Can you describe it?"

Luke blinked his eyes closed, partly to call up the memory and partly to conceal his tears from Rupert. He tried to picture Rupert's phone four nights ago, when they were at dinner and a man's face had appeared on the screen. The shape was indistinct. He squeezed his eyes tighter, and the facial features became clearer. A sound began to resonate in his ears. It was a voice. A voice speaking to him.

Luke shook his head and opened his eyes. "It's a man's voice," he said. "I don't know whose, but it's the same guy each time. And he's telling me to do something. Something I don't want to do. But he's making me do it."

Rupert sat up, a look of excitement on his face. "What does he make you do?"

Luke shook his head. "I don't know. I can't hear the words. It's just a feeling. A real bad feeling."

He moved closer to Rupert, who wrapped an arm around him, and kissed him.

"You've made progress," said Rupert. "You okay?"

"I feel great," Luke said quietly. "But if I keep making progress, maybe one day I'll no longer be this waif and stray who needs nursing. Will you still stick around for me then?"

Rupert gave a deep, contented sigh and held Luke tightly in his arms.

"You've turned my life upside down this week," he said. "Do you want to know something? I was all set to quit the BBC and go to work for CNN in Atlanta for an obscene amount of money. Well," he added after a moment's thought, "it would probably have been an obscene amount of money."

"You'd leave London?" asked Luke, his head resting on Rupert's chest. "For Atlanta?"

Rupert sighed. "Not this week. And probably not next week either." He kissed Luke on the head. "Life's just got interesting again."

LUKE STOOD at the open doorway and looked in. The room was in shadows, lit only by the hallway light behind him. At the far end, he could see two high-backed armchairs on either side of a large fireplace. There had been a fire lit in the grate earlier, but it was now mostly ash. The remaining wood was charred, with only a few orange glows and wisps of smoke. Indistinctly in the shadows, he thought someone was sitting in the armchair to the left of the fire. He could just make out a pair of legs, stretched out.

"Come in, Luke," said the man in the armchair without looking around. "You're late."

Luke held back. He had no idea he had an appointment with anyone. He thought he knew the voice but could not place who it was.

"Come in," said the man again. "We have a seat prepared for you."

Luke entered the room. He walked to the armchair on the right of the fireplace and stood with his hand resting on its back. He looked to his left, but the high wing of the man's chair obscured his face.

"No, not that one," said the man. There was a hint of irritation in his voice. "We've got the special one for you. Remember? It's just for you."

Hands grasped Luke's shoulders, and his arms were forced behind his back. He struggled, but the two men on either side of him were too strong. They pushed him away from the fireplace, back to the middle of the room where a large black chair sat. He was sure it had not been there when he first entered. The men turned him around and forced him to sit in the chair. One of the men pinned him down, and the second secured him with a wide leather strap around his waist. More leather straps bound his wrists, forearms, calves, and ankles. Hands grasped his head, and a final strap was secured around his forehead.

"That's better," said the voice from beside the fireplace. "You know how important this is, don't you? For you and for your family. It's far better if you don't resist. You'll only bring shame on yourself."

A large pair of headphones now covered Luke's ears, and the voice sounded deep inside his head.

"We'll begin," said the voice. It was deep, resonant, slow, and deliberate. "What you'll experience will not be pleasant, but you must be cleansed. We can do that, but you must work with us. If you don't and this fails, they'll have no choice but to use the alternative." The man sighed. "And the family doesn't want that. It would be such a loss. Your mother would be distraught."

A large television screen was wheeled in front of Luke. The screen glowed into life, and Luke could see the image of a man and a woman holding hands. The image was replaced with one showing the same couple kissing. This happened several more times with images of different couples.

A picture of two men holding hands appeared on the screen, and Luke felt a strange tingling sensation in his forearms. With difficulty, he peered down at them. The leather strap holding his head against the back of the chair restricted him, but he could see wires had been attached to his forearms. The tingling sensation stopped. He looked up at the screen. The image had been replaced with that of a man and a woman holding hands. It stayed on the screen for several seconds before being replaced with a picture of the same two men. This time they were kissing. The tingling sensation in his arms was much stronger. Painful. Luke fought hard against the leather straps, but he could not break free.

"Don't resist, Luke," said the voice in his head. "You'll only make it worse."

Luke tried to close his eyes, but his eyelids were held open by some kind of clamp. The image on the screen grew bigger. At the same time, the pain in his arms grew even stronger. His whole body shuddered with the intensity of the pain. The image on the screen was not only growing larger, but the entire screen was moving toward him. He strained his arms against the leather straps that secured them, and his neck felt ready to break as he pulled against the strap holding his head. All the while, the pain in his arms grew more severe.

In terror, he yelled out, "Stop it! Stop it. Please! Stop it!"

He felt hands grasp his shoulders and the weight of a body on top of him. He tried to push hard against it and found his arms were now free. He flailed about, hitting the man who sat astride him.

"Luke! Luke! Wake up!"

The voice was like a shock of cold water. Luke opened his eyes to see Rupert sitting on his chest. He held Luke's shoulders down against the bed, and there was a look of panic on his face. Luke blinked several times and stopped flailing his arms. He was exhausted, and his chest heaved as he fought to catch his breath.

Rupert relaxed his grip on Luke's shoulders, collapsed, and rolled to lie alongside Luke.

"Don't do things like that," said Rupert. He wrapped his arm over Luke's chest. "You scared the life out of me."

The two men lay in silence for several minutes. Rupert massaged Luke's shoulder as Luke's breathing settled back into a regular rhythm. Finally, Rupert spoke.

"Can you tell me about it now?" he asked quietly.

Luke took Rupert's hand in his and kissed it. He rolled onto his side to snuggle back into Rupert's embrace. The two men curled into each other, and Rupert's arm wrapped reassuringly around Luke's waist.

"It scared the shit out of me," said Luke. "It was like the scariest horror movie you've ever been to. And then some. There was a man sitting in an armchair with his back to me. In a room somewhere."

"Did you know the place?" asked Rupert. He pressed his mouth close to Luke's ear. "Have you been there before?"

Luke shook his head. "I don't think so. It was a big room. In an old house. There was a fireplace. Old, heavy furniture. Then they strapped me to this chair and attached electrodes. I was being tortured. Electric shocks—"

"Fuck," said Rupert. "No wonder you were screaming. Who were they?"

Luke shut his eyes and tried to see his dream again. But it was fading rapidly. He struggled to picture the room and the men in it. The room was dark, and the faces of the men were indistinct. Luke concentrated hard on the fireplace. He remembered now. There were candleholders on either side of the fireplace. Each one held three candles, and the candles in them had almost completely burned down. They flickered and guttered as they struggled to remain alight. Above the fireplace, illuminated by the sputtering candlelight, was a picture in a frame. There was something about the picture. It was large and imposing, and the frame was ornate and gilded.

Luke sat up and turned to Rupert. "I gotta get my portfolio case. I gotta draw it. I can see something now, but it's fading rapidly."

He climbed out of the bed and ran down the stairs to the small living room of the cottage. His portfolio case was where he had dropped it by the front door. He picked it up and ran back up the stairs to the bedroom. Rupert was sitting up in bed and had turned on the bedside light. Luke sat on the end of the bed and unzipped the portfolio case. He pulled out a pad of paper and some pencils and began to sketch rapidly.

"That's a sight I don't think this old cottage has ever seen," said Rupert. He knelt behind Luke and looked over his shoulder at the emerging image on the sketchpad. "A naked artist running up the stairs at two in the morning." He rested his chin on Luke's shoulder and nibbled his ear. Luke's pencil darted across the surface of the sketchpad.

After several minutes, Luke leaned back against Rupert and stared at what he had drawn. Was it from his dream, or was it from a long-forgotten memory? The two seemed inextricably intertwined. On the paper, he had sketched the gilt frame of the picture. Within the frame was a shield, across which was a chain, broken in the middle. Something like a lightning bolt arose from the break in the chain. A long, curved banner beneath the shield bore the words Libe Uni VA.

"Shit, Luke," whispered Rupert in his ear. "I know what that is."

He jumped off the bed, reached for his mobile phone, and began typing. He carried the phone over to the window and stared at the screen with increasing frustration.

"Shit, shit, shit," he said and waved the phone above his head. "Why can I never get a bloody signal in the countryside? It's like the nineteenth century down here."

He lowered his arm and looked again at the screen. His face took on a look of triumph, and he turned the phone around for Luke to see. "That's what you've drawn. The lettering's incomplete, but it's clear. That's the crest for the Liberated University. It's in Virginia."

Rupert walked back to the bed, sat down beside Luke, and put an arm around his shoulder. "That university is linked with a series of suicides here in the UK." He squeezed tight on Luke's shoulder. "I don't think that was a dream you had, my beautiful American," Rupert went on. "Some bastards actually did that to you. The question is, who?"

CHAPTER 24

THE AFTERNOON sun burned down relentlessly on the brown, parched lawns at Pendley House. Lying under the shade of a willow tree, close to the small stream that crossed the estate, Luke was pleasantly exhausted by the heat. He had stripped to the waist and wore a pair of faded khaki shorts Rupert had lent him. His head rested on Rupert's chest, and he stared up into the canopy of the willow tree. Rupert's arm lay across his chest, his thumb hooked into the waistband of Luke's shorts.

"Is it always this hot in Britain?" asked Luke, batting away a wasp drawn to the remains of their picnic. "I thought it rained a lot."

"Oh no," said Rupert. "We're a tropical country really. We just put these stories of lousy weather around to keep the crazy Americans out."

Luke rolled over to squat astride Rupert. He grabbed Rupert's arms and pinned them to the ground. "Well, you failed with this particular crazy American." He inclined his head to kiss Rupert's bare chest. "You'll have to find another tactic to get rid of me."

Rupert wriggled free from Luke's grasp and started to tickle him around the waist. Luke fell back on the grass and pulled his knees to his chest. His face was contorted with laughter.

"No, no!" he cried. "I surrender. Anything but that."

Rupert relented. He rolled over and laid his head on Luke's chest. Luke reached down and gently massaged Rupert's nipple.

"Oh wow, I don't think that's a good idea," said Rupert, and he exhaled deeply. "Not this close to the house, anyway. You know what that does to me. What if Mother hears?"

Luke turned to look at the rear of Pendley House. It was a huge, Victorian gothic structure, with extravagant, castellated walls and turrets at either end of the building. A vast conservatory, probably built in the twentieth century, opened onto a veranda. This led to a formal garden and then to the lawns on which Luke and Rupert lay, close to the stream.

"It's nearly a hundred yards to the house," protested Luke. He turned back to Rupert. "Are you getting bashful, Rupert Pendley-Evans? And I thought you were such an experienced man. Then you go all coy as soon as Mom and Pop are nearby."

Luke took Rupert's nipple firmly in his fingers and began to massage it. Rupert groaned in appreciation and grasped Luke's wrist.

"No, no," said Rupert again. "Not here. I just don't think they're quite ready for all this yet."

"Oh, I don't know," replied Luke. He intertwined his fingers with Rupert's. "Your mom's been real sweet to me today. She chatted and asked me about stuff—"

"What stuff?" asked Rupert.

"Oh, you know. Where I'm from. And what I do. How long we've known each other, and whether we're going to have kids—"

This time it was Rupert who rolled on top of Luke. He placed his arms on Luke's chest and rested his head on them. "You can't joke about stuff like that. Not the way my parents are. I'm sure Mother's still waiting for me to 'grow out of my little phase.' As she'd probably put it."

Luke reached forward to kiss Rupert, then lay back on the grass and gazed up at the willow branches. The tree's green leaves dappled the blue of the sky.

"I wouldn't be so sure," replied Luke after a moment of contemplation. "She seemed pretty cool with me today. I like her. She might be more modern than you think."

"Modern?" Rupert sat up. "Modern? You've got to be kidding. Nothing's modern in Middle Claydon. You're trapped in ye olde England here, my dear deluded American." Rupert stood up and held out his hand to Luke. "Come on. Let's go for a walk. I'm going to show you something."

RUPERT PUSHED open the gate and gestured Luke through. They entered the churchyard, and Rupert closed the gate behind him. The late-afternoon sun reflected off the yellow sandstone of All Saints Church and gave it a look of burnished gold. The two men paused to admire the building. A square tower at the east end had a castellated top and buttresses at either corner. The main body of the church extended to the west. There were narrow, slit-like windows and a shallow sloping roof.

"Gee, it's beautiful," said Luke.

"This is why I could never think of Mother as modern," said Rupert. "This is part of our heritage. And she's fiercely proud of it."

"Well, she sure should be. I'd guess thirteenth century? Maybe fourteenth? Post Norman anyway. The start of European Gothic. What the Victorians tried to copy five hundred years later."

Rupert looked at Luke and raised his eyebrows. "You know your stuff."

"Yeah, well," replied Luke. "Don't assume all Americans are dumb when it comes to history. Come on. I wanna see inside."

"One of the advantages of being part of the Pendley-Evans family," said Rupert as they arrived at the imposing oak entrance door of the church, "is that we have keys to the churches around the estate." He pulled a large black wrought iron key from his pocket and inserted it in the lock. "That's strange. Seems like I didn't need it. Someone must be here already."

He pushed open the heavy door, and they stepped into the church.

The sudden drop in temperature as they entered contrasted with the late-afternoon heat. Luke shivered. The building smelled of floor polish and mustiness. Like a secondhand bookstore. A shaft of light flooded through the west window and glinted off the golden cross and candlesticks on the altar ahead of them.

"Oh my," said Luke. "This is something else."

"I was christened in this church," said Rupert. "So was every generation of my family. It's actually part of the Claydon House estate. My family was too poor to have its own church—"

"You gotta be kidding," said Luke.

"Well. More likely too mean," acknowledged Rupert. "This church was originally adopted by the Verney family. They've been in Middle Claydon since the sixteen hundreds—"

"Wow," said Luke. "I guess that beats you guys."

"Oh yes. The Pendley-Evanses are new money by comparison. My many greats grandfather made his fortune from slavery in the eighteenth century. He bought the farm, I guess, to try to gain respectability."

"No shit?" said Luke. "What's it like to be the descendant of a man who exploited my ancestors?"

Rupert shrugged. "Not great. But there's not a lot I can do about it. By contrast, the Verneys were good people. I'll show you."

He closed the door behind him and led Luke down the central aisle of the church. They walked past rows of wooden pews until they reached one near the front. Rupert stopped and invited Luke to sit. Rupert sat alongside him and pointed to a plaque fixed to the pew opposite.

"That's where Lady Verney would have sat with her husband, Sir Henry Verney. He was a liberal Member of Parliament for this area in Victorian times. And alongside them would sit Lady Verney's sister, Florence Nightingale."

"You mean the Lady with the Lamp?" asked Luke. "No way."

"That's right. The founder of modern nursing and the Red Cross was a regular here."

"Is it true she was gay?" asked Luke.

Again, Rupert looked at Luke with astonishment. "Your history's amazing." He leaned back against the pew. "It's difficult to say. Lesbians didn't officially exist in Victorian Britain. The Victorians refused to believe a woman could love another woman. But in Florence's writings, people say she made it pretty clear she loved women."

Luke put his arm around Rupert's neck. Rupert turned, and Luke kissed him slowly on the lips. "Thank you, Rupert," he said. "This is just so perfect. I really don't want this to end."

"And it doesn't have to," said Rupert. He kissed Luke again.

"There you are, darlings," said a voice from the front of the church. "Are you boys having a nice time?"

"Oh bloody hell," Rupert gasped. "Mother must be here with the flower committee."

Luke followed his glance to the altar. Rupert's mother had brought in a large armful of flowers and placed them on the floor. Rupert stood up and stepped into the aisle of the church.

"Come on," he whispered to Luke. "I really don't want to stick around."

"Oh, don't be like that," Luke whispered back. "She's just being friendly."

"I'll just finish arranging these," said Lady Pendley-Evans in a loud voice. "Then we can walk back together."

"No way," Rupert hissed in a low voice.

"Don't be so mean to her," Luke said. "She's trying real hard to be friendly." But Rupert ignored him and stalked back down the aisle of the church.

Lady Pendley-Evans looked up when the main door slammed shut.

"Oh dear," she said. "Rupert's in an awful hurry again. Luke, darling. Could you possibly give me a hand with these? The vases are terribly heavy."

Luke stood and joined her by the altar.

"You know," said Lady Pendley-Evans. "Rupert is being most awfully silly about all this. I've watched you two today. Rupert's the happiest I've seen him for years." She turned to Luke and fixed him with a clear, unblinking gaze. "You're the best thing that's happened to my son in a long time."

Luke was taken aback. He had not expected to hear this from Rupert's mother.

"Lady Pendley-Evans—" he began.

"Please call me Cynthia. We really don't need to be so formal."

"Cynthia," Luke corrected himself. "Rupert thinks you don't approve of him for—"

"Being gay?" asked Cynthia. "Oh, that's ridiculous. Like all mothers, I just want my son to be happy. Rupert's father and I took a dim view of his gallivanting around, sowing his wild oats hither and thither. But maybe you can finally bring some common sense and stability into his life."

Luke laughed. "Gee, I never thought I'd hear myself being described as someone who could bring common sense—"

"Why on earth not?" interrupted Cynthia. "You seem like a sensible fellow. Rupert needs to settle down."

"But Rupert was angry because you didn't want us to sleep together in the house last night—"

"Oh, what a lot of nonsense." Cynthia's laugh was hearty and deep, like a man's. "I remember when Clarence and I were courting. The last thing we wanted was to sleep in the big house with his ghastly parents. What if they'd heard us having rumpy-pumpy?"

Luke could not believe his ears.

"Don't look so surprised, young man," said Cynthia. "We might be dried up old prunes now, but Clarence and I could go all night in our younger days. We always stayed in the old cottage. So much more sensible. Clarence is awfully noisy in the bedroom department. That's why I put you two down there rather than in Rupert's room."

She knelt to pick up a long iris stem and began to strip leaves from the lower part of its stalk. "Now be a dear and fetch me one of those large vases over there." She peered up at Luke and gave him a knowing look. "We can let Rupert have his little sulk while we have a lovely chat together, can't we?"

LUKE RETURNED to the cottage at six thirty that evening. Rupert was in the living room, drying himself with a towel after his shower. His mobile phone was on the mantelpiece, and it played a bluesy rock track. Luke paused to admire the sway of Rupert's hips as he danced.

"Hey," said Luke. "Nice action."

Rupert turned. There was a sheepish look on his face. "I'm sorry about earlier. I shouldn't have walked out like that. But meeting Mother in the church rather caught me off guard—"

"Hey, hey," said Luke. He walked over to Rupert and hugged him tight. "Mmm, you smell good." He kissed Rupert. "Don't worry about it. As for your mother, she and I have been doing some real good talking."

Luke released Rupert. He stood in front of him and put his hands on his hips. "Now it's your turn to talk to your mother. No arguments."

Rupert visibly twitched. Luke looked down at Rupert's growing erection and back to Rupert's crooked smile. "Looks like I need to be strict with you more often." He leaned against the back of the couch, folded his arms, and shook his head. "But I'm afraid that will have to wait until later. There's no time like the present for talking."

"What on earth have you two been cooking up?" asked Rupert.

"You'll find out. But don't worry. It's all good. Now go get some clothes on. I'll come up to the house in a while."

Rupert kissed Luke and disappeared up to the bedroom. Ten minutes later he returned in a pair of tan chinos, a slightly crumpled white shirt, and a pair of loafers.

"Well, that could do with ironing," said Luke. He straightened Rupert's collar and tried to smooth out the worst of the creases in the shirt. "Maybe Cynthia will do it for you."

"Cynthia?" asked Rupert. "My, my. You are getting on well with Mother. You've got me worried now."

He reached for his phone from the mantelpiece.

"Could you leave that?" asked Luke. "I don't know this album you're playing, and I really like it."

"You've never heard Fleetwood Mac's *Rumours*?" asked Rupert. "You're kidding me, right? This is only the best British rock band of all time."

Luke shrugged. "Put it down to amnesia. Or maybe it never got to America."

Rupert laughed. "Oh, it got there all right."

He hugged Luke. The two men kissed and held each other's heads in a fond embrace.

"Oh, I'm going to enjoy introducing you to so much good stuff," said Rupert. He walked to the cottage door. "I guess this amnesia thing has its benefits after all." And he slammed the door behind him.

Luke took the phone, sat on the couch, and looked at the screen. It was playing Fleetwood Mac's "The Chain." He was still nervous the screen might trigger another attack. But he took a deep, calming breath and flicked through the names of the other tracks listed on the album.

The music was cut short when the phone began to ring and vibrate in Luke's hand. He looked at the screen and saw the name

Christian. As he tried to decide what to do, he let the phone ring. On the fourth ring, he pushed the Answer button.

"Hi," said Luke. "Rupert's not here, but—"

"Hello, Luke," said the voice in his ear. "You need to listen to me very carefully. I'm going to tell you what you must do. And you will do everything I say."

CHAPTER 25

THE EVENING sun shone through the tall beech trees ranged along the side of the footpath, and they cast long shadows. Rupert walked up the path toward the side entrance to Pendley House. He stopped to watch sheep in a distant field settle down for the night. A lone pheasant about fifty yards distant swooped across in front of him and hid itself in the cover afforded by the ancient hawthorn hedge bordering the field.

Rupert tried to anticipate what his mother could possibly have to say to him. Perhaps she was won over by Luke's charm and gentle manner. If so, Luke had worked remarkably quickly. Rupert thought back to his visit the weekend before. His mother had been her usual, critical self. Rupert had been particularly tired after a grueling series of night shifts in the newsroom. But his mother had dismissed it as being the result of his "usual gallivanting around the sordid fleshpots of Soho." He had spent much of the weekend in his bedroom, partly sleeping, partly avoiding his parents.

Rupert resumed his walk and arrived at the side door to Pendley House. "Evening, Mother," he called as he entered the large scullery off the main kitchen. "I've come to give you a hand with supper."

Lady Cynthia Pendley-Evans peered around the open kitchen door into the scullery. She had a pair of reading glasses perched on the end of her nose. They were attached to a chain around her neck, and she wore a large black-and-white striped apron.

"No you haven't," she said. "You're here because Luke told you we should have a little talk."

She turned from the doorway and stood with her back to him at the large wooden table in the middle of the kitchen. "Although, now you're here," she said, without turning around, "you can scrub some potatoes for me. I'm making a potato salad to go with the gammon."

Rupert entered the kitchen and crossed to the stove. Steam rose from a large pan containing a huge piece of gammon, and the rich aroma of spices filled the kitchen.

"Where's Jeanette?" asked Rupert.

"I've given her a few days off," replied his mother. "Her sister's arrived from New York, and they need to spend some time together."

She turned and looked over her glasses at Rupert. "And don't look at me like that, darling. I can cook, you know. It's just because you and your father were always so critical of my cooking that I preferred to leave it to Jeanette. The potatoes are in the cupboard over there."

Rupert could not remember the last time he had seen his mother cook. It was a pleasant surprise to see her in the kitchen. But he resented the guilt she had directed at him. He could not recall being critical of her cooking in the past. But then it must have been a long time ago. He unhooked a large pot from above the stove and carried it to the sink to fill with water.

"Don't keep me in suspense," he said. "What do you want to talk about?"

"Oh, darling, you are funny," said his mother. "I want to make sure you're going to carry on seeing Luke, of course."

Rupert set the pan of water on the stove with a clatter and lit the gas. He turned and leaned against the worktop with his arms folded. "I have no idea. Does it bother you?"

Lady Pendley-Evans put down the large knife she was using to slice tomatoes and looked at him over her glasses.

"Stop being so defensive, darling," she said. "I asked a perfectly simple question. He's a charming young man. Your father and I would be very happy to see you two together—"

"Father would?" asked Rupert. "I can't believe that for a second."

"And why the devil not?" said a voice from the hallway. Rupert's father appeared at the kitchen door, a bottle of gin in his hand.

"Ready for a snifter, old girl?" he asked Lady Pendley-Evans. He looked across to Rupert. "What are you drinking, my boy? Gin and it, or are you going straight to wine?"

"I'll have a gin and tonic, thank you, Father," replied Rupert. "Can I help with them?"

"No, no," replied Lord Pendley-Evans. "You stay with your mother. And tell her why you think I'm such an old fart."

"I didn't say that," protested Rupert.

"No, darling," said his mother. "But we know that's what you think of the pair of us."

"Well," said Rupert, "I have some reason to." He pulled a bag of small earth-encrusted potatoes from the cupboard and tipped them into the sink. He began scrubbing fiercely with a brush to remove the soil. "You've made it very clear for years that neither of you approve of me being gay."

"Don't take it out on the potatoes," said his mother. "They'll have no skins left if you carry on like that." She picked up her knife and resumed slicing the tomatoes. "And you're being grossly unfair. Of course, we were rather shocked when you sprang it on us. But that's fourteen years ago. Please bless us with a little intelligence to have thought about it since then."

Rupert set down his scrubbing brush and turned to look at his mother. "Then why haven't you said anything before?"

"The subject never arose," replied Lady Pendley-Evans. "Whenever I've asked you about your life in London, you've told me very little. I learn more from the *Daily Mail* about your night life than I do from you."

Rupert laughed. "No wonder you don't approve of me, if you believe what you read in that rag."

"Darling," said his mother, "it's not that I don't approve of you—"

"Well, maybe a little," interrupted his father. He entered the kitchen and set down a tray of drinks on the table.

"Don't interrupt, Clarence dear," said Lady Pendley-Evans. "It's not helpful." She turned back to Rupert. "I'm worried about you, Rupert darling. You go to all those dangerous places with your work. We see you on the television in Yemen or Iraq or somewhere equally terrifying. The next moment we read about you in the newspapers, flitting from one nightclub to another. Then once in a blue moon you come back here and spend the whole time being grumpy."

She took the drink her husband offered her, and tasted it. "Heaven."

Lady Pendley-Evans took off her glasses and looked at Rupert. "I just want to know when you're going to settle down and be happy."

"And we'd like to think," added his father, "that this young chap might be the one to do it."

Rupert could scarcely believe his ears. He stared at Lord Pendley-Evans with his mouth open.

"And don't look at your father like that," remonstrated his mother. "You stopped doing your ghastly goldfish impersonations when you were seven, thank God."

Rupert accepted the tall glass his father handed him and drank from it. He was grateful Lord Pendley-Evans had been generous with the gin.

"When did you change your mind about me being gay?" asked Rupert. "Because I know damn well you hated 'having a poofter for a son,' as you so charmingly put it."

"Yes, well," said his father. He coughed loudly. "I suppose I've had a few years to think about everything—"

"It helped a lot when Roger told you he had a boyfriend," added Lady Pendley-Evans.

"Roger?" said Rupert with incredulity. "Your school friend who was in the Guards? You never told me."

"Well, you never asked."

"Why on earth would I ask you if Roger was gay? Why would it ever cross my mind?"

"I thought maybe you chaps had a sixth sense about these things," said his father. "Because I certainly didn't. Mind you, he seems very settled with Jeremy. So it's all for the best."

Rupert considered responding to his father's assumption about his gaydar but decided it was better not to react.

"And their wedding this spring was absolutely heavenly," said Lady Pendley-Evans. "All those beautiful young men in uniform. I simply swooned."

Rupert turned to his mother. "All right. How do you explain me away at All Saints these days? Are you still telling them I'm waiting for the right girl to come along?"

"Oh, don't be so silly." Lady Pendley-Evans put her glasses back on and resumed preparing the salad. "Reverend Whittaker left years ago. The Reverend Kenneth might be a little progressive for your father's tastes, but I find him charming. And it's so convenient that his partner is the organist and choirmaster."

Rupert nearly dropped his glass. "The vicar of All Saints is gay?"

"I'm sure I've told you," said his mother. But Rupert was certain she had not. "He's so charming. And he's marvelous with the flower committee. Anyway. You haven't answered my question. Is Luke the one?"

Rupert was speechless. Partly because of everything he had just learned from his parents. But mainly because he was unsure of the answer to his mother's question.

"I really don't know, Mother," he said at last. "We've known each other for such a short time—"

"That's got nothing to do with it," interrupted his father. "I knew with your mother the moment I laid eyes on her. As soon as I asked her to dance, she was the girl for me."

"And I knew I wasn't going to get any better than your father," said Lady Pendley-Evans. "He was quite a catch that season. Luke seems to be a lovely young man. And he's very smitten with you. Are you smitten with him?"

Rupert set down his glass and leaned back against the sink. He thought back over the last few days. He had never felt so happy in his life.

"I suppose I am," he said. "But Luke's got a lot of problems in his life."

Lady Pendley-Evans crossed the kitchen to where Rupert stood. She put her arms around his waist and reached up to kiss him on his cheek. "My darling boy. We all have heaps of problems. Life's like that. But they're so much easier to face when you're with someone who loves you. I think he could be very good for you."

"Hey, hey," said Rupert. But he could not help smiling. "Aren't you rushing ahead just a bit? Let me take things at my pace. It's been a very eventful week."

"Of course, darling." She patted his chest and looked up at him. Her face wore the same expression he remembered when she came into the nursery to say good night when he was a boy. "And when the time comes, Reverend Kenneth will be very happy to offer his blessing on you both."

"Mother," said Rupert. "Just...." He put his arms around her waist and hugged her. "Hold your horses, eh?" Rupert dropped his arms and wiped his eyes. "But thank you."

He turned to his father. "Both of you. I wasn't expecting to hear any of this tonight. And as for the vicar of All Saints—"

He was interrupted by a loud thumping on the front door.

"Who the devil's that?" asked Lord Pendley-Evans. He put down his drink as the banging on the front door sounded again. "All right, all right, I'm coming as fast as I can." He stomped off to the hallway, followed by Rupert.

Standing on the doorstep was Christian. He looked past Lord Pendley-Evans to Rupert. "Thank God I've found you. Where's Luke?"

"What on earth are you doing here?" asked Rupert. "I brought Luke here to get him away from London. Just like you said. What's happened?"

"It's Pa," replied Christian. "I think he's tracked him down. He wants to kill him."

CHAPTER 26

RUPERT RAN down the footpath to the cottage. Christian followed close behind, and Lord Pendley-Evans brought up the rear at a slower pace. The sun had almost set, and it was getting dark. The way back seemed more threatening and forbidding than Rupert's relaxed walk less than an hour earlier.

He arrived at the door of the cottage and threw it open. "Luke!" he called. "Where are you?"

There was no answer. Rupert checked the bathroom, then ran up the stairs to the bedroom. There was no sign of Luke. Rupert hurried back down to the sitting room.

"He's gone, Christian," said Rupert. "Are you sure it's your father? Do you think he's taken him?"

Before Christian could reply, Lord Pendley-Evans arrived, breathless and panting heavily. "Let's go back to the house and get the dogs," he wheezed. "They'll track him down. Have you got a piece of Luke's clothing? It will give them his scent."

Rupert picked up a T-shirt Luke had draped over the back of one of the chairs. The three men ran from the cottage and headed back to the house. Halfway up the footpath, they met Lady Pendley-Evans. A man was at her side, and he held the leads of two hounds that trotted in front of them.

"I managed to find Frank," said Lady Pendley-Evans. "And Jeanette's back at the house calling the police." She pointed to the dogs with her walking stick. "We thought you might need the boys."

"That's my girl," wheezed Lord Pendley-Evans. "Always thinking two steps ahead."

Rupert bent down. The hounds ran up to him and wagged their tails. He held Luke's T-shirt before them. The two dogs sniffed it and whimpered as they did. Lady Pendley-Evans knelt down alongside the animals and whispered in their ears.

"Jasper! Jack! My beautiful boys," she said. "Go find!"

The dogs lowered their noses and sniffed the ground. They circled the area for several minutes before they shot off in the direction of the cottage. The humans followed behind. At the cottage, the dogs sniffed around the front porch and pawed at the front door. Lady Pendley-Evans's commanding voice cut through the evening air.

"Jasper! Jack! To ground, boys! Hunt!"

The dogs lowered their noses once more and explored the outside of the cottage. The hound with the red collar was the first to move. He found a fresh scent and followed his nose along the path to the back of the cottage.

"Good boy, Jack!" called Lady Pendley-Evans. "Go on, Jasper. Follow!"

Jasper picked up the scent and rapidly caught up with Jack. The two dogs trotted side by side along the path, their noses close to the ground all the way.

"They're heading for the barn," said Rupert. "That's got to be where they're going."

He and Christian followed the dogs down the path. After fifty yards, the path opened out into a farmyard in front of a large metal barn. The heavy main doors were closed, but light streamed from a low open doorway to the right. Rupert saw the shape of a man silhouetted in the entrance. The dogs began to bark excitedly. The man turned at the sound and immediately ran off.

"Oh dear Lord," said Christian to Rupert. "It's Pa."

"You go after him," said Rupert. He turned to Frank. "And you go with him. I'm going to check the barn."

Frank bent down and released the dogs from their leashes. They ran off into the darkness, barking. Frank and Christian followed behind. Rupert strode up to the doorway and stood on the threshold. At the far end of the barn stood Luke with a long wooden ladder.

"Luke," called Rupert. "Thank God. Are you all right?"

But Luke said nothing. He carried the ladder toward the middle of the barn and leaned it against a low beam. It was as if he had not heard Rupert. Luke had a coil of rope slung across his shoulder. He set his foot on the bottom rung of the ladder, checked it was steady, and began to climb.

"Luke," Rupert called again. This time Luke paused and looked across to him. Still he said nothing. Lady Pendley-Evans appeared at Rupert's side.

"What's the matter with the boy?" she asked. "He seems to be in his own little world."

Rupert ran to the ladder and placed his hand on Luke's shoulder. Luke kicked out hard, and his foot connected with Rupert's groin. The pain was instant and eye watering. Rupert fell back to the ground, winded.

"Shit," Rupert cried. "It's me. What the fuck's the matter with you?"

Luke stared at him silently with cold, empty eyes. He turned back to the ladder and once more began to climb. Rupert scrambled to his feet and wrapped his arms around Luke's legs. Luke kicked violently, but Rupert clung on grimly and used his weight to try to dislodge Luke from the ladder.

Lady Pendley-Evans reached up with her walking stick and brought it down hard on Luke's hands. His fingers slipped and lost their grip on the rungs of the ladder. Luke fell backward, and Rupert let go of his legs. He rolled to the side to avoid Luke as he fell to the concrete floor of the barn. Rupert turned to see Lady Pendley-Evans stride over and raise her walking stick above Luke's head.

"No!" Rupert called out. Lady Pendley-Evans paused, the stick frozen in midair. Luke shook his head and scrambled to his feet. He grabbed the stick from Lady Pendley-Evans's hand and brought it down hard on her shoulder. Rupert watched, horrified, as his mother fell back. He lunged forward, grabbed the walking stick from Luke, and threw the American to the floor. The two men rolled until Rupert was on top, using his hands to pin Luke's shoulders to the ground.

"Stop it, Luke," said Rupert. "Just stop it."

Beneath him, Luke panted heavily. He struggled to lift his shoulders. His head strained forward, and his eyes were wide with terror.

Rupert held firm, and Luke's struggles subsided. He stared at Rupert, and it was as though his eyes gradually refocused. The look of terror was replaced with one of recognition. His shoulders sagged to the floor, and he released a long, exhausted sigh.

"What have I done?" he said. "What have I done?" His shoulders shook, and tears trickled down his cheeks. "It's all my fault."

Rupert leaned forward and kissed Luke on the lips. "We know it's not your fault."

Luke opened his eyes. "I'm so sorry. I told you I was too complicated. I've fucked it all up, haven't I?"

Rupert kissed him again. This time long, and slow. Their lips parted, and Rupert saw a look of defeat in Luke's eyes. "I love you, Luke," he said. "You've been through a terrible ordeal. But it's all over. I'll protect you from now on."

Luke wrapped his arms around Rupert and hugged him tight. "And I love you too, my beautiful Englishman."

"Well, that's all bloody fine" came the voice of Lord Pendley-Evans from behind them. "But what about your bloody mother?"

Rupert sat up and looked across to Lady Pendley-Evans. She had drawn her knees to her chest and was trying to stand. There was a thin trickle of blood running down her neck from a head wound. Rupert jumped off Luke's chest. He went over to his mother, knelt down, and rested a hand on her shoulder.

"Mother!" he said. "Don't get up. You're injured."

"Oh fuck," said Luke behind him. "What have I done?'

"Don't worry, young man," replied Lady Pendley-Evans. "Just a flesh wound. Had worse coming off a bally horse, you know." She sat down heavily on the floor, and her body swayed.

"Must say, though," she continued. "Feeling a bit woozy." She looked at Luke. "Damn fine right arm you've got there. Do you play tennis?"

Luke stood and walked over to kneel beside Rupert. "I'm real sorry, Cynthia. I didn't know what I was doing just then."

Lady Pendley-Evans held on to Rupert's arm to steady herself and fixed Luke with a hard stare. "Well? Do you play tennis?" she repeated. "We need a decent doubles partner around here." She looked up at Lord Pendley-Evans, who was standing beside them. "Isn't that right, Clarence? We're getting fed up with thrashing the locals. They're no bally good at all."

Before he could reply, there was a commotion at the entrance to the barn. Rupert turned to see Christian and Frank shove a tall, elderly man through the doorway. The man stood with his head bowed. Frank held the man's arms firmly behind him. In the distance, Rupert heard the sound of several police sirens.

"We found him trying to break into the Jaguar, my lord," said Frank.

"Who the devil is he?" asked Lord Pendley-Evans.

Rupert turned to Luke. The American's eyes were open wide with terror. Rupert put his arm across Luke's shoulders. He was shaking with fear.

"It's your father," said Rupert. "Isn't it, Luke?"

LORD PENDLEY-EVANS entered the main reception room at Pendley House. He held up a whiskey bottle and waved it at Rupert.

"Another snifter, old boy?" he asked.

Rupert shook his head. He sat on one of the large couches alongside the fireplace with Luke in his arms. Christian sat on the couch opposite, a glass of water in his hand. The doors to the garden were open, and the night breeze filled the room with a heady scent from the roses in the flowerbeds that lined the veranda.

"Your mother's sleeping," said Lord Pendley-Evans. "Snoring like a trooper."

"I wish she'd gone to the hospital," said Rupert. "She ought to have that head wound looked at."

Lord Pendley-Evans waved his hand dismissively. "No need for any fuss. Jeanette bandaged it for her. She'll be right as ninepence in the morning."

He sat down on the couch opposite Rupert and Luke and poured himself a large whiskey. He turned to Christian alongside him and raised his glass. "Cheers, old boy." He took a long drink from the glass. "Now, young man. You've got a few things to explain."

"I've told the police everything," said Christian. "Pa forced me to tell him where Luke was hidden. He's always had this power over Luke and me."

He turned to Rupert. "I wanted to call you to warn you. But Pa had taken my mobile phone. So I came up here to find you."

Lord Pendley-Evans snorted dismissively.

"You knew Luke was in danger," said Rupert. "You've known for a while. That's what you warned me about this week. Why haven't you ever told the police?"

Christian shifted in his seat. He looked down at the glass of water cradled in his lap. "I just thought Pa wanted to treat him. I didn't think he was going to go that far."

"Treat him?" asked Lord Pendley-Evans. "Treat him for what?"

"For his sexuality," replied Christian. He continued to look down at his glass. "We needed to convert him."

"We?" asked Rupert. "You mean, you were in on this too?" He held Luke tighter in his arms. "He's your brother. What the fuck were you thinking of?"

"The Family Council says that those who are homosexual are evil and sinful. But they can be converted to their natural sexual nature—"

"You don't believe that nonsense, do you?" asked Lord Pendley-Evans. "Good God, man. Where do you think you are? Seventeenth-century Salem? We don't burn witches in England any longer, you know." He took a drink of whiskey. "Neither do we punish decent young men for loving each other and doing what comes naturally to them."

Rupert looked at Lord Pendley-Evans with astonishment. His father was full of surprises this weekend. He turned back to Christian.

"So just what exactly was your involvement in all this?" he asked. "Luke's been tortured, hasn't he? I guessed that from the nightmare he had the other night. What did you use? Electric shocks? Branding irons?"

Christian shook his head vigorously. "I had nothing to do with that." He looked at Rupert. There were tears in his eyes.

"But you knew it was happening, didn't you?" asked Rupert.

Christian avoided Rupert's glare and lowered his head again. "I knew something was happening." He took a drink from his water and lowered the glass. Staring into it as if he might find his courage there, he began to speak.

"It was last January. Two o'clock in the morning. I got a call from the emergency room. Someone had found Luke. He was about to hang himself from a tree on the grounds of the university. They cut him down and called 911. When I got to the hospital, he'd lost his memory. He didn't know who I was."

He looked over to Luke.

"I love you, brother," he said. Tears were trickling down his face. "I never meant for all this to happen." He sniffed and wiped his eyes with the back of his hand. "When I found out what they were doing," he continued, "I brought you to London. I gave you a new identity. I've got plenty of money. I set you up in the apartment."

Luke sat up and leaned forward. "A new identity? My name isn't Luke Diamond, then?"

Christian shook his head. "I only changed your last name. Your Christian name is Luke. But you're not Diamond. You're a Matthews, like me."

"So is it you who pays money into my bank account?" asked Luke. "And pays the bills for Dr. Ballantyne in Harley Street?"

"Yes," replied Christian. "She's the best in the profession they say."

Luke thought for a moment. "Did you set me up with the exhibition at that gallery?"

"You're a wonderful artist," said Christian. "I hoped it might help bring your memory back." A note of pride sounded in his voice. "And the gallery wouldn't have wanted to exhibit your work if they didn't think it was good."

Luke sighed. "I don't understand you. You did all that. And then, in another breath, you say I'm evil and sinful." He stood up and looked down at his brother. "Do you think I'm evil? Do you think I'm sinful?"

He turned to Rupert and held out his hand. Rupert stood and wrapped his arm around Luke's waist. The two men turned to face Christian. "Do you think," continued Luke, "that because we love each other, we must be sick? That we must be cured? Christian, I'm your brother. Answer me."

Christian didn't respond at first. He lowered his head and his shoulders shook. Tears fell into his lap. Then...

"I don't know anymore" was all he said.

CHAPTER 27

RUPERT CARRIED the large package into the living room of Luke's apartment and put it down on the table.

"It's the post, Luke," he called. "There's a package just arrived for you."

The parcel was about two feet square, three inches thick, and weighed a couple of pounds. Rupert turned the package around on the table and examined its brown-paper wrapping for evidence of where the parcel had come from. There was no address for the sender and no postmark to betray its origins.

Luke entered the living room and crossed to the table. He had a towel wrapped around his waist and another slung around his neck. He kissed Rupert and picked up the package.

"Well. I know it's not my birthday," he said. "And I don't remember ordering an expensive present for you." He turned and kissed Rupert again. "So I wonder what's in the mystery package?" He put it back on the table and headed for the living room door.

"But first, coffee." Luke went into the kitchen, opened a cupboard, and took out two cups.

"I don't believe you!" said Rupert. "You can't keep me hanging in suspense like this." He tore at the wrapping of the parcel, only to reveal further packaging inside.

"Hey, hey!" called Luke from the kitchen. "That's mine." He dropped the cups on the counter, hurried back to the living room, and made a grab for the parcel.

"Oh no," said Rupert, holding the package above his head. "You didn't want to open it. So it's mine now." He continued to tear at the packaging, and shreds of paper rained down from his hands. Luke grabbed Rupert around his waist and began to tickle him.

"That's not fair," cried Rupert. He dropped the package, bent forward, and wrapped his arms around Luke's shoulders. He kissed Luke on the lips, and the American's tongue ventured into his mouth. Rupert pulled back and rested his hands on Luke's waist.

"Wait, wait," he said. "We've got all the time in the world for that." Rupert bent down, picked up the partly unwrapped parcel from the floor, and handed it to Luke. "I'm sorry," he said. "I hope I didn't damage it when I dropped it." Luke kissed him one more time and carried the package over to the couch. Rupert followed and was about to sit next to Luke when the doorbell rang again.

"Busy day," he said. "I wonder if that's the postman with more gifts for you."

He walked down the hallway and opened the front door.

"It's not too early, is it?"

"Rosalind," said Rupert to the pathologist. "What are you doing here?"

"Well, I'll go away again if you don't want me here," said Rosalind, a note of irritation creeping into her voice. "But I thought you'd be interested in the developments since your little shenanigans up at Pendley House two nights ago."

Rupert stood aside and gestured with his hand. "Please come in. We're about to make some breakfast."

"Oh, not for me," said Rosalind. "I'll just have a cigarette." She entered the apartment, walked down the hallway, and waited by the living room doorway for Rupert to catch up.

"And you must be Luke," said Rosalind. She turned to Rupert, and as if confirming a diagnosis to a fellow doctor, said, "Now I understand."

"Understand what?" asked Luke. He stood and tightened the towel around his waist, looking self-conscious.

"Why Rupert was so desperate to leave my offices when you called him the other day," said Rosalind. "If I was straight, I'd feel the same. I'm his doctor friend who chops up bodies for a living, by the way." She walked across to Luke and held out her hand in greeting. "Rosalind Goodman. Since your ordeal at Pendley House two days ago, I've learned a great deal about the fate you've just narrowly avoided." She shook Luke's hand firmly and looked over to the open doors that led onto the balcony. "Oh good," she continued. "Let's go outside. I'm desperate for a smoke."

"Do you want some coffee?" asked Luke. "I was just about to make some."

"Of course," she said. "Strong and black."

Rosalind walked onto the balcony and lit up a cigarette.

Rupert turned to Luke. "I'm so sorry. It's just how she is."

Luke laughed. "I'm getting to like your family and friends. They're a great deal more honest than mine." He walked to the kitchen door and turned. "And certainly more direct."

Rupert followed Rosalind outside. A cloud of cigarette smoke enveloped him, and he began to cough.

"You've struck gold there," said Rosalind. She ignored Rupert's discomfort. "I'd hang on to that one if I were you."

"Thank you for your advice, Rosalind," choked Rupert. He leaned over the rail of the balcony to inhale the clearer air. "Okay. Tell me what you've found."

Rosalind drew deeply on her cigarette and held the smoke in her mouth for several seconds before slowly exhaling.

"They're bastards," she said finally. "I've been talking to your chum Jerry at the National Crime Agency, and he's got a pretty clear picture of what they were up to. We've got a nice exclusive for you. But you're going to have to get your skates on. All the other newshounds are sniffing around."

She leaned with her back against the balcony, the cigarette between two fingers. "They're called the Real Family Council." She paused for a response, and when none was forthcoming, asked, "Heard of them?"

Rupert shook his head.

"Bunch of puritanical primitives with too much money," continued Rosalind. "They believe people like you and me are evil. That we need to be converted"—Rosalind used her hands to mimic quotation marks in the air—"from being gay. It's called gay conversion therapy. They use fake science to justify its effectiveness." She sniffed haughtily. "I've never read such a load of rubbish in my life. It's been going on for decades. They use aversion therapies. Which means they show you pictures of activities they believe to be evil and give you electric shocks. Or they give you chemicals to make you throw up. They've been claiming it cures you of being gay. It's all bollocks, of course. In the seventies they even used to give people ice-pick lobotomies. Bastards."

She took a final drag on her cigarette, stubbed it out on the balcony railing, and flicked it over the edge.

"Well, this Real Family Council took it to a whole new level," she continued. "Their fake doctors admit the aversion therapy is a waste of time. But they still think we're evil. So they simply brainwash their victims and make them go and kill themselves instead."

Luke emerged onto the balcony with a tray. His towel had been replaced by a pair of sweatpants and a singlet. He set the tray down on a narrow table.

"Lovely," said Rosalind. She picked up the coffeepot and filled one of the cups. "I'll be mother." She handed the cup to Luke. "Your father was one of the directors of the Real Family Council. I'm sorry to have to say it, but it's unspeakable what he's done." She poured a cup for Rupert and one for herself.

"How did they think they could get away with it?" asked Rupert.

"Oh, in America they were very well-connected," said Rosalind. "They had people at the highest level covering up for them. The mistake they made was trying the same thing in Britain. They had a few powerful supporters, of course. But not enough, thankfully."

Luke sighed and rested his head on Rupert's shoulder. "I feel so responsible."

"Oh my dear boy, don't be so foolish," said Rosalind. "How on earth could you have known what your father was up to? And what was he thinking of? To actually want to kill you. His own son. I can't begin to imagine how you must feel right now."

"I don't think it's really sunk in yet," Luke replied. "I still feel kinda numb." He turned to Rupert. "Come inside. I've got something to show you."

Rupert followed Luke back into the living room. A large photo album was laid open on the table.

"That's what was in the parcel," said Luke. "I guess Christian sent it."

Rupert thumbed through the album. Happy faces looked back at him from photographs on every page. The album began with the wedding day of Luke's parents. It told the story of the birth of each of their four children, up until their teens. Rupert turned to Luke.

"Is it triggering memories for you?" he asked.

Luke shook his head. "It doesn't feel real at the moment. It's like looking at someone else's family. They're not my brothers and sisters. Not my parents." He turned to Rosalind, who had entered the living room and stood beside them. "Will they ever become my memories?"

She shrugged. "I'm no psychiatrist. All I can say is, I think it's bloody fortunate you're alive. You're the best thing that's ever happened to Rupert."

Luke grinned. "People keep saying that." He turned to Rupert. "Is it true?"

Before Rupert could answer, the doorbell rang again. And he threw up his hands. "It's like Piccadilly Circus this morning." He headed for the front door.

"Mornin', sweetheart. Did ya miss me?" Sandra reached up, kissed Rupert on both cheeks, and pushed past him into the hallway. "Where's my sexy American?"

As soon as she spotted him, Sandra ran down the corridor, threw herself at Luke, and wrapped her arms around him.

"You better not go anywhere again soon," she said. "We need to keep a close eye on you from now on."

She gave Luke another hug and turned to Rosalind. "I'm Rupert's picture editor, love. Sandra Giles. Rhymes with piles. Who are you?"

Rosalind stared down at Sandra with a look somewhere between horror and disdain. She glanced at Rupert, who stood at the entrance to the living room. "Is this the one you keep complaining about? I can see why."

Rupert shook his head and walked over to Sandra. "Sandra, this is the pathologist, Dr. Rosalind Goodman."

"Oh yeah, I remember," said Sandra. "You're the dodgy dyke he used to manage the London Pride parade with. What is it about dead bodies with you?" She shuddered. "Gives me the creeps."

She turned her back on Rosalind, stood between Rupert and Luke, and put her arms around them.

"I've got a little request for you two," she said. "Now that you're not going to be needin' the apartment, I was just wonderin'—"

"What do you mean not needing the apartment?" asked Rupert.

"Well, surely you're not goin' to be staying down there?" asked Sandra. "Not when you've got your gorgeous Yank to sleep with up here. Then again, if you decide to take that job in Atlanta—"

"Oh no," said Rupert and shook his head. "I don't think I'm going to Atlanta for the foreseeable future. And there was nothing ever definite about the job with CNN."

"Oh, it's definite all right," said Sandra. "My mate Donna—you remember? The one who was at the Tavern the other night? The one what's moved to CNN? She said it's an open secret the job's definitely yours. With or without Beverley fuckin' Daniels."

Rupert shook his head again. "I can't go to America just now. Not after everything that's just happened to Luke. Maybe in a couple of years—"

"No," Luke interrupted. "Of course you should take it. This is the break you've been waiting for. Don't turn it down on my account."

"But I can't leave you until all this gets sorted out," protested Rupert. "What about your therapy sessions with Dr. Ballantyne? You're going to need a lot of support after all this. I'm certainly not going anywhere just now."

Sandra tutted loudly and looked up at Luke. "Oh, dear. He really doesn't get it, does he? They've got shrinks in America, haven't they? I 'eard they 'ad more shrinks than bleedin' lawyers. Why don't the pair of you go and leave all this behind? It's the perfect opportunity for both of you. A new start."

Rupert looked at Luke, whose eyes were twinkling with mischief.

"She's right," said Luke. "You don't rate Dr. Ballantyne very highly anyway. The question is, will you take this waif and stray with you?"

Rupert put his hands gently on either side of Luke's head and gazed into his eyes.

"I'll take you wherever you want to go," he replied and kissed Luke on the lips.

"Oh, for fuck's sake," said Sandra. "Get a room, you two."

DAVID C. DAWSON is an award-winning author, journalist, and documentary maker living near Oxford in the UK. He writes about men in love—facing danger and solving crimes. In 2017, David was an award winner in the President's Awards for Adult Suspense and Thrillers.

David joined the BBC in London and worked in radio newsrooms for several years before moving to television as a documentary director. During the growing AIDS crisis in the late eighties, he is proud to say that he directed the first demonstration of putting on a condom on British television.

He has lived in London, Geneva, and San Francisco, but now prefers the tranquility of the Oxfordshire countryside. He produced videos for several charities, including Ethiopiaid, which works to end poverty in Ethiopia, and Hestia, a London-based mental health charity.

David has one son, who is also a successful filmmaker. In his spare time, David tours Europe on his aging Triumph motorbike and sings with the London Gay Men's Chorus. David is most proud of the time they sang at the House of Lords, campaigning for equal marriage to be legalized in the UK.

Website: www.davidcdawson.co.uk
Blog: blog.davidcdawson.co.uk/#home
Twitter: @david_c_dawson
Facebook: www.facebook.com/david.c.dawson.5
LinkedIn: uk.linkedin.com/in/davidcdawson
Email: contact@davidcdawson.co.uk

Featuring David C. Dawson

ONE

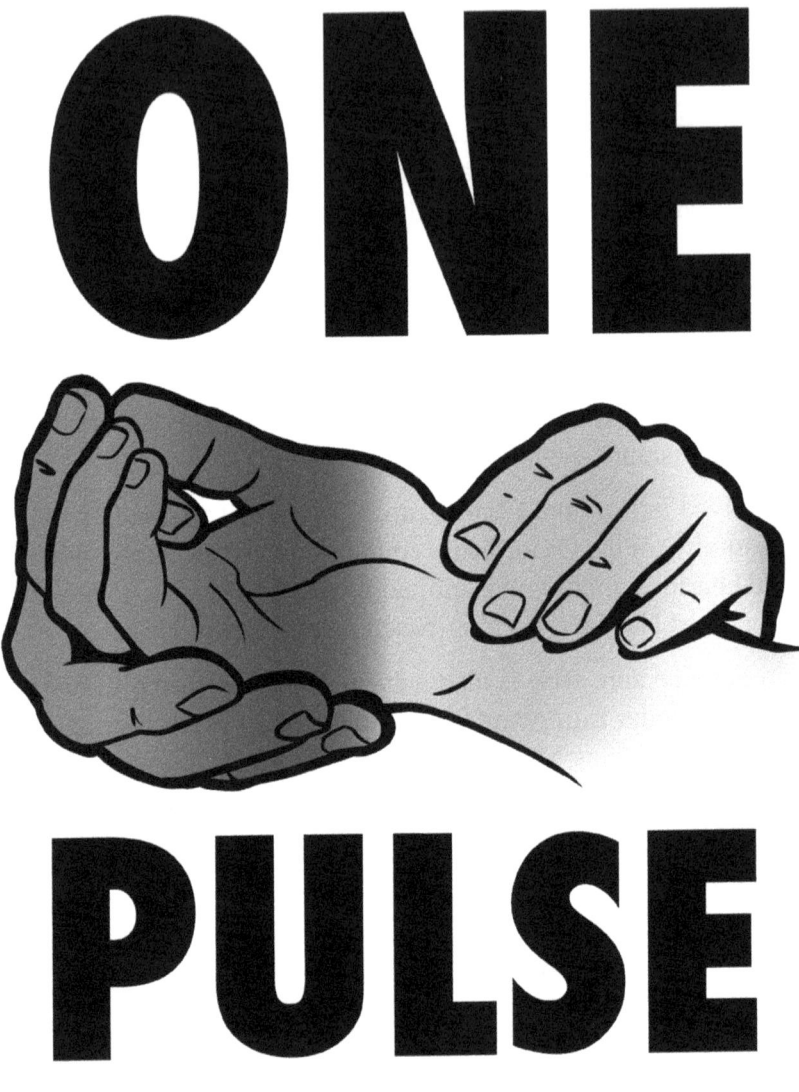

PULSE

A ꓷREAMSPINNER PRESS ANTHOLOGY

Stories drive life. Sometimes life is good; sometimes life is bad. But it's the nature of our community that in the aftermath of an act of hatred, we respond with love. Because darkness cannot exist in the presence of light. Cruelty cannot stand against compassion. Negativity will never overcome hope.

To show our support for those affected by the Orlando shooting, our authors, editors, artists, and staff have volunteered their talents to create this anthology. All proceeds will be donated to LGBT organizations in central Florida. Join us as we celebrate the triumph of love over every obstacle.

www.dreamspinnerpress.com

FOR **MORE** OF THE **BEST GAY ROMANCE**

DREAMSPINNER
PRESS
dreamspinnerpress.com